THE BOY
WITH WINGS
CLASH OF THE SUPERKIDS

Other books by Lenny Henry

The Boy With Wings

The Book of Legends

CLASH OF THE SUPERKIDS

MACMILLAN CHILDREN'S BOOKS

Lenny Henry

Illustrated by Keenon Ferrell

THE BOY WITH WINGS
CLASH OF THE SUPERKIDS

Published 2023 by Macmillan Children's Books
an imprint of Pan Macmillan
The Smithson, 6 Briset Street, London EC1M 5NR
EU representative: Macmillan Publishers Ireland Ltd, 1st Floor,
The Liffey Trust Centre, 117–126 Sheriff Street Upper
Dublin 1, D01 YC43
Associated companies throughout the world
www.panmacmillan.com

ISBN 978-1-5290-6789-7

Text copyright © Lenny Henry 2023
Illustrations copyright © Keenon Ferrell 2023

1 3 5 7 9 8 6 4 2

A CIP catalogue record for this book is available from the British Library.

Printed and bound by CPI Group (UK) Ltd, Croydon CR0 4YY

To all the readers everywhere: thank you.

Keep on reading.

Prologue

Tunde Wilkinson was soaked to the skin and, for a *BRIEF* second, he had no idea why.

Then he sank. And sank again. Each time, he would desperately flap and kick and flail until his head broke the surface once more. He sucked in air and tried not to panic. Thoughts **skittered** across his mind. *What is this? Where am I?* He floated momentarily, looking around. He was in a room filled with rapidly rising water. This was a nightmare.

The water had almost reached the ceiling. There was just enough space in which he could snatch a breath. And then there was frenzied movement as he flapped his wings uselessly and a mini wave crashed over his head, submerging him completely. For that brief moment, as he struggled and kicked, attempting to make his way back to that life-giving quarter of an inch of air, he saw others just like him flailing, splashing, trying to surface, but most of them were succumbing to the weight of water and sinking fast. Tunde had been submerged for so long (Seconds? Minutes? Hours? Days?) the pressure was beginning to tell on his body. He was panicking.

In a brave attempt at survival, he flapped his wings slowly underwater and kicked his legs and arms and wings and managed to scrabble his way to the top. He inhaled air from the narrow gap and then one final slosh of unforgiving water washed over him and formed a seal and there was no more air to be had. The ceiling was gone. They were all completely submerged now and unless he grew gills, there was no hope of survival.

Tunde held his breath for as long as he could. His heart beat out of his chest. His lungs were bursting and he felt his wings growing **HEAVIER** and **HEAVIER** and **HEAVIER**. His brain began to fizz and get tired from the lack of oxygen and a stray thought filled his mind: *Why am I being tested like this?* And then there was a slow realization: *This isn't a test – this is an ordeal.* If he'd been on dry land, he would have felt endless tears pouring down his cheeks. But he was underwater, and so, he felt nothing. He closed his eyes. Everything went **BLACK** . . .

There was an abrupt shaft of light!

And then Tunde felt himself being shaken vigorously. He sat up and sucked in long lungfuls of air! HE WAS ALIVE!!!

Tunde's mum, Ruth, was staring at him, a worried look in her eyes, the overhead lights in his room suddenly on.

'You all right? I heard you scream. Were you having a bad dream?'

Tunde looked at his mum, embarrassed that she'd seen his nightmare panic. 'I'm fine. Stupid dream, that's all.'

On her way out, she pointed to the alien nightlight on his bedside table. 'Do you want me to put this on?'

Tunde snorted with derision. 'I'm not a baby, you know.'

Ruth laughed, turned off the lights and left the room, shutting the door gently behind her.

Tunde tossed and turned a little bit, thumping pillows and rearranging his blankets. Finally, he gave

up, turned on the alien nightlight and just sat there muttering to himself.

'Stupid dark – why would I be scared of the dark? It's only *dark*. It's nothing. Darkness is rubbish! Humph!'

And he punched the pillow several times and thumped his head down into them. And as he lay there, he thought to himself that, actually, he *did* sound like a big baby . . . and eventually drifted off into a dreamless sleep.

1

The summer holidays in Ruthvale were usually a mixture of rain, sleet, snow and hail – and that was day one. After that, the weather in the south Midlands behaved as though it were playing peek-a-boo with a tiny baby. Today, however, was a **glorious** day in Ruthvale, where the rain held off for at least five minutes every so often to let the watery sun peek through the inky clouds that hovered above like black-clad bodyguards outside the local disco.

Usually, mud-spattered, rain-drenched kids would play in the puddles on the high street, reading the signs in the windows: 'Staff unwanted' or 'Half-day opening, most days' or 'Teeth whitening on credit (happy to work tooth by tooth, see Vera for details)'.

People would normally crowd onto buses and into their cars at this time of year, off on their holidays, whether it was Cyprus or Skegness, Brazil or Bradford. There were only two words that mattered right now to every single young person in Ruthvale: No School.

But there was much more than that on the mind of thirteen-year-old Tunde Wilkinson. For today, Tunde felt anything but glorious.

See, Tunde had a secret that was more mahooooooooosive than a blue whale balancing on top of a woolly mammoth holding up a Titanosaur who was carrying the Friday night big shop with one claw and a large anvil with the other. Tunde had recently discovered that he wasn't just a Black kid from the Midlands with a beaky nose; he was the Boy with Wings! Yes, real wings!

Tunde was actually the chosen leader of an entire war-like alien race, the Aviaans, but had been raised on Earth by his adoptive parents, Ron and Ruth Wilkinson.

Despite his birth father being a warrior leader, Tunde had been brought up to be kind, considerate and thoughtful, which meant he didn't fly around at super-high speeds b-doinging off people left and right just to get in the front of the queue at the pictures.

The only people that knew Tunde's secret were his mum and dad and his best friends: Nev, Kylie, Jiah, Dembe and Artie.

Nev was a promising footballer, with slightly bow legs, dreadlocks and a comprehensive knowledge of banging **choooons** and almost incomprehensible street slang.

Kylie was smart, kind and very in touch with her (and everyone else's) emotions. Her mother was a *therapist* and had written books like **'Your Behaviour Stinks'** and 'Tell your Inner Child to Shut Up!' She loved archery and could shoot the jockey shorts off a fly at a hundred paces.

Jiah was a tip-top mathlete, bound for a high-ranking university somewhere soon in her future (so her parents had told her repeatedly since birth). But, recently, ever since she'd flown into space with Tunde to battle the crazy cat people (remember that?), she'd been more interested in the possibility of **spooky alien alternate dimensions than advanced algebra.**

There was Dembe too (a talented footballer and future fashionista). A while ago, she'd been adopted by Tunde's mum and dad, and, while that had caused a bit of a COMMOTION in the Wilkinson household, her life nowadays was much more stable. Though one thing that remained unpredictable and was always changing was the colour of her hair! Tunde couldn't keep up.

Yellow and red or orange with stripes and now, for a moment at least, black with pink polka dots!

Another new addition to the Wilkinson family was Artie Fisher, a ridiculously clever AI robot. Tunde's parents had built him at their workplace, **The Facility**; a top-secret science complex on the edge of town. Artie had been created to protect Tunde while he was at school and record his vital signs (blood pressure, excitement levels, hydration, as well as his emotions). This had got just a bit out of hand and led to a giant robot freezing everybody in the school and challenging Tunde to a fight (see *Attack of the Rampaging Robots*). Artie had been based at home ever since.

The only other person in the whole of Ruthvale (and the rest of the world) who knew about Tunde's powers was Professor Krauss from **The Facility**. He might look in his early fifties, but from his references to times when TV was on just three channels and a man called Churchill ran things, Tunde and his mates secretly thought he was waaaaaaaay older than that, so either he was using an excellent moisturiser or he was drinking a 'make me look like Harry Styles' anti-ageing smoothie on the down-low each morning. He was also probably the smartest person in a five-hundred-mile radius of Ruthvale (sorry, Jiah!) and he led the team who found the alternate dimension that Tunde's parents came from.

But right now, Tunde felt separated from everybody he knew. His parents had just told him that he would *not* be going to **Land of Adventures** – aka the **best holiday park on Earth** (just up the M1, near Nottingham) with all of his friends as planned. Land of Adventures was an enormous play park, featuring laser games, rollercoaster rides, ginormous swimming pools, **super-long twisty, turny** water slides, virtual reality games, music, and an endless supply of sugary food and foot-long vegan hotdogs. It was the super-mega-dope place to be this summer. All his friends had booked tickets ages ago, packed their bags and, now, they had gone.

'This is just not fair!' Tunde complained to his

parents. 'Why do we **have** to go to this **stupid** thing in London?'

His mother glared at him beadily. 'Because Professor Krauss said, "Tunde's involvement in this programme could be the best thing that's ever happened to global security." Do I have to say more?'

'But it's the summer holidays. I want to be with my friends!' Tunde begged.

'It's going to be a very exciting couple of weeks,' Dad said. 'And you're gonna make us *all* proud.'

'We're sorry, Tunde,' his mum added, 'but, trust me, it's even more worthwhile and exciting than Land of Adventures.' Tunde wasn't sure that was possible.

Professor Krauss had told a colleague from an American research institute about Tunde's abilities and also about that time when he saved the world (see *The Boy with Wings* Book 1). So instead of letting him visit the Land of Adventures with all his mates, his parents had made the decision that Tunde should instead go and meet this mysterious scientist.

Grumpily, Tunde agreed and left that morning

with Mum and Dad to head to the big city.

As soon as they all arrived at Birmingham New Street station to catch their London-bound train, they found Professor Krauss waiting for them. He led them to a secret platform, behind a door that said 'VERY PRIVATE – DON'T EVEN THINK ABOUT COMING IN HERE. YES, I MEAN **YOU**'.

Professor Krauss told Tunde everything he could remember about Professor Abigail Shapiro. Apparently, she was known as the 'BIGGEST BRAIN IN BOSTON'. She had degrees in Biology, Physics, Astrology, Astronomy, Psychiatry, Advanced Mathematics and Super-Advanced Mathematics and O.M.G. This is Difficult Next Level Mathematics . . . phew. When she was a teenager, the world's so-called smartest people would leave messages on her answerphone for advice: 'Yes, but why **DOES** G equal squiggly line times a banana divided by infinity symbol?'

Professor Krauss had first met her at a conference in Washington DC called 'The Bermuda Triangle, Extraterrestrials & Superhumans – Can't we all just get along?' Professor Krauss had spoken about all the work they were doing at **The Facility** (although he didn't mention the talking silverback gorillas who had teamed up, tunnelled their way out of **The Facility,** stolen a trio of trucks, driven to Heathrow Airport and then hijacked a jumbo jet to Rwanda). And then Professor Shapiro made an even more brilliant speech about her work with superhuman kids who could be trained to protect the world.

Professor Krauss was so impressed by her speech, he'd stopped her afterwards and told her about his work with Tunde. She was intrigued and they made an arrangement to meet at the beginning of the summer at a super-secret laboratory in London called **The Complex,** which was why Tunde was now sulking opposite his parents in the First-Class compartment of a private train carriage (attached to the 8:43 from Birmingham New Street) *whizzing* its way to London rather than shooting down a super-slide with all his best mates.

'You could look a bit more excited about meeting

the smartest person in the world, Tunde,' his mum said.

'Er, excuse me,' said Professor Krauss, looking a bit offended.

Tunde's dad interrupted hastily, coming to everyone's rescue, 'What we need here, my amigos, is JOKES. A fella walked into a pet shop and said, "Can I buy a wasp?" The shopkeeper said, "We don't *sell* wasps." The bloke said, "You've got one in the window . . ."'

Tunde laughed.

Encouraged, his dad continued, 'What do you call a woman who sets fire to all her bills? . . . Bernadette!' He raised both hands in triumph and did a little dance.

Ruth shook her head in mock disbelief and suddenly there was a PING!

Ron glanced at his phone and then **HOWLED** like a wolf. 'Yes! We got the tickets!'

'Tickets for what?' Tunde said.

'*Les Misérables.*'

Tunde didn't understand why they'd want to go and watch a show that sounded like it was invented to make him feel even grumpier. He listened as his mum and dad rabbited on about all the things they were going to do in London: the sales were on and Mum wanted to go to a very posh department store (Dad had bought her a £10 voucher for Christmas). Meanwhile, Dad was excited to attend a show at Kew Gardens about mutated vegetables. 'There's a potato the size of a pineapple, and a pineapple the size of a pumpkin, and get this, a pumpkin the size . . . of a potato!' Only Tunde's dad could sound *THIS* excited about manky fruit and veg. His parents **wouldn't** stop going **on** and **on** and **on** and **on** about 'reconnecting' to London, the place where they fell for each other all those years ago ♥ (**yuck**). *Thankfully*, this lurve-fest was interrupted by Tunde's phone ringing loudly.

It was a video call from the gang!

Nev, Kylie, Jiah and Dembe appeared on his phone screen, all wearing Laser Blaster Probe T-shirts and wielding unfeasibly sized *super-soaker* water pistols. Nev was completely drenched and looked the happiest Tunde had ever seen him.

'Ah Tunde, this place is lit! You should be here, bruv. There was this banging music festival last night called **BADABLAPS!** MC Erfkwake was on and he did **"Louder dan a Hurricane".** My head nearly *exploded!* I love that choon!'

Jiah jostled into the frame. 'Tunde! There's a graphic novel library here. There's everything from The Adventures of Peculiar Pete to Earwig Boy! They even have early issues of Super Intelligent Goddess Girl! I am in heaven.'

Dembe was performing complicated flick flacks in

the background and yelling at the top of her voice over and over, 'See that? See THAT? SEE THAT?'

Meanwhile, Kylie totes caused havoc with her nine-gallon super-soaker. She was a crack shot and almost everything Tunde could see looked as though it had been dunked in the nearest canal – Nev's phone included!

Before Tunde could respond and talk about his rubbish holiday destination, Nev interrupted, 'Listen, bruv, we know you're busy on the train going to wherever it is man's goin', so we're gonna let you get on, yeah? We got sixteen different types of vegan sticky chicken wings at lunch to get through, yeah? So we gonna bounce, cuz – laters.'

Then everything went blank and they all disappeared. Tunde looked at his disappointed reflection in the screen. This was going to be the **Worst. Summer. Ever.** He screamed inwardly. Then he groaned outwardly and said, 'Ugh, this is going to be terrible.'

He had absolutely no idea how right he was about that.

Tunde walked up to Professor Krauss, who'd moved to the other side of the carriage to take a Zoom call. On the professor's laptop screen, Tunde could see a laboratory technician in a white coat who stood next to a large water tank containing a rather irate dolphin.

'Ah, Tunde,' said Professor Krauss kindly. 'Come in, we were just finishing.'

The dolphin interrupted, '*You* might have finished, but *I* was only just getting started – the living conditions here are—'

Professor Krauss snapped the laptop shut and the screen went blank. 'Sorry about that. Our robo-dolphin is quite the diva. What can I do for you?'

'I'm not sure I want to go to this **Complex** place,' Tunde said. 'Can't it wait until next year? I want to be with my friends.'

Professor Krauss could see Tunde was upset – not because he was crying or making faces, but mainly because, as he looked out of the window over Tunde's shoulder, he could see and hear several hundred incredibly cross crows, rooks and ravens **squawking, shrieking** and **cacaaawing** as they sped alongside the train.

The professor smiled and said, 'You might want to practise those breathing techniques we went through. Remember, your feelings affect every bird in the vicinity.'

Tunde turned and saw the multitude of angry birds desperately trying to keep up with the train.

'Ooops.'

He took a deep breath and counted to ten, just like Kylie, who *was all about the zen*, would've suggested, and the birds quietened down and peeled away.

Professor Krauss's phone went off, and Tunde could overhear the robo-dolphin, even angrier, complaining about his lodgings.

'I'd better leave you to it.'

He walked back to the other side of the carriage to hear his dad singing 'You've got to pick a pocket or two' from *Oliver!*

Tunde smiled despite himself.

'Look, our son is smiling! That's more like it!' His mum reached out and hugged Tunde tight.

'All right, all right.' Tunde laughed. 'Mind the wings. I'll be using them all week!'

Dad laughed and said, 'Right, my son, it is now time for ... The Joke-a-Palooza.'

The Joke-a-Palooza was something Dad had invented. For as long as they could manage, they went back and forth, sparring with jokes, puns and silly one-liners.

Dad started, 'Two guys stole a calendar ... they got six months each!'

Mum followed, 'I was in the canteen at work the other day. I said, "There's no chicken in this chicken soup" and the dinner lady said, "There's no horse in the horseradish either."'

Tunde, who was finding it hard not to laugh at

these terrible jokes, said, 'I went to get a haircut the other day. The barber said to me: "Would you like your hair cut round the back?" I said: "Is there no room in the shop?"'

On and on it went until Professor Krauss came over to see what all the noise was about.

'It's Joke-a-Palooza, Professor,' Tunde explained. 'Have you got a good one for us?!'

Professor Krauss raised an eyebrow. 'I went to a party on the moon once. It was terrible – absolutely no atmosphere.'

Mum and Dad looked at each other. Tunde looked out the window. The only laughter came from the cawing of the crows outside.

Professor Krauss cleared his throat and tried again. 'Why do you go to prison for throwing sodium chloride at somebody? It's a-salt.' He paused for effect. 'Get it? *Assault?*'

Tunde groaned.

Dad raised his hands and said, 'I've got a good one. Why **didn't** the skeleton cross the road?'

Ruth looked at Tunde, who looked at Professor Krauss, who waited with pursed lips.

Ron hitched up his trousers and said, 'Because he didn't have the guts!'

Unfortunately, Mum had just taken a sip of fizzy pop. She laughed so hard she SQUIRTED some out of her nose. Professor Krauss put his face in his hands and laughed for quite a long time.

Ron strutted around the carriage. 'You give in or are you thirsty for more? I've got another one—'

Thankfully, just then a whistle blew.

'Come on, you lot. Let's get the luggage together. We're coming into Euston now.'

Tunde pulled his bag down from the rack and almost fell over as the super-fast train switched tracks.

An automated voice asked them to strap their seat belts in and hang on to their hats if they were wearing them. Suddenly, their carriage disconnected from the train, hopped onto another track and then *shot* almost straight downwards into a tunnel at high speed. After this sheer drop, the train absolutely, no word of a lie, I swear on your dead goldfish's life, **CORKSCREWED** for the last 300 metres of its journey before **_screeching_** to a halt perfectly in front of its secret and final destination.

'Oh my gosh! That was the best ride ever. That was sick!'

Dad had turned bright purple. 'I think I'm going to be sick.'

Mum passed him a soda and he opened it gratefully, but was sprayed by an outburst of FIZZ which got him right in the face! Tunde, Professor Krauss and Mum all laughed uproariously.

In all the corkscrewy CHAOS, Tunde's bag had been tossed around the carriage and his clothes had spilled everywhere. He went searching for his jumpers and jeans and found a pair of Math Sox, which Jiah gave him for every birthday and Christmas whether he liked them or not (he did not!). They were covered in different equations and numbers, stitched in silver and gold. Tunde didn't think he needed maths in his **LIFE**, let alone on his socks. But Jiah thought they were super mega cool. Tunde thought they were about as cool as a vindaloo pizza washed down with a pint of molten lava but was glad to have something that reminded him of his friend anyway.

The doors opened and a smartly dressed lab technician drove up in a state-of-the-art golf buggy. Once they'd loaded on their stuff and sat down, the technician **shoooomed** towards computerized doors, which opened on their approach and took them further into the bowels of the building.

Tunde was amazed at how much space there was. Who knew there were all these secret compartments, caverns and caves underneath London?

Professor Krauss explained, as if reading his mind: 'After the war, the world leaders who had been fighting for peace wanted us to have key spaces dotted around where the world's cleverest people could work, discuss and experiment on matters of great interest to world peace. **The Facility** was one of them and **The Complex** another.'

Tunde looked around. They had passed through

several doors and were now approaching a magnificent shiny lift, which opened silently to greet them. 'Wow! This is like Admiral Splod's Warship in Space Rampage. All **his** doors *ssh* open like this.'

And they did.

They reached their floor and, as the doors *shhhhh'd* open once more, they revealed a tall woman who introduced herself.

'My name is Professor Abigail Shapiro. Welcome!' she exclaimed.

She smiled and shook hands with everybody. She had light

29

brown skin and straight, dark brown hair piled high on her head. She wore a long white coat, but she didn't look like a stuffy, boring scientist. She looked stylish. Her wrists jingle-jangled with bangles and her nails were painted red and gold. She'd lodged a pencil into the middle of her bun and she carried a computer tablet in one hand. Her smile lit up the room.

'You must be the Wilkinsons. It's such an honour to have you here at **The Complex.** We've sorted you tickets for *The Lion King*, *Phantom of the Opera*, and,' she grinned, 'that one about cats, I've forgotten its name.'

Ron answered her straightaway. 'Oh, you like a joke, do you? How do we know Saturn was married more than once?'

'Because it has too many rings?' Professor Shapiro parried back.

'OK, you are a smart one,' Ron said.

Professor Shapiro offered a joke of her own: 'What did the oak tree wear to the pool party? Swimming trunks!'

No one laughed at that.

'Never mind,' she grinned tightly. 'This is where we say goodbye,' and the two professors watched as the Wilkinsons hugged each other and said soft words of departure.

Mum held Tunde very tight and whispered in his ear, 'Just try your hardest, that's all you can do – you'll be fab.'

Dad held on to Tunde hard and said, 'And if *anyone* tries it on with you, just give them a big bonk on the beezer.'

Ruth looked at him sternly – 'We won't be doing that here. We'll be making friends and talking and working with each other, won't we?'

Tunde nodded. 'Absolutely – no punching or kicking anyone, at any time!'

They all hugged again, and then, with Professor Krauss offering his hand for a grown-up handshake, which Tunde took and then shook, they all disappeared on another golf buggy which carried them upwards to ground level and away to London and all its charms.

Tunde was now all alone.

Professor Shapiro led the way to the lift which descended many floors even deeper into the earth. If it weren't for the super-cool air-conditioning, Tunde thought they might start feeling the heat of the earth's core. However deep it was, he certainly had no phone signal.

Finally, the doors opened and Tunde's jaw dropped. They had arrived at the top of a central eight-sided tower. There were large computers, thousands of screens, big leather-bound books, high-tech workstations, a bubble gum machine, a jukebox, a very comfortable-looking chair shaped like a baseball glove and so much more. There were windows on each side of this tower, which overlooked a sprawling array of interconnecting rooms and spaces large and small – this was obviously where everyone worked, rested and played. Tunde thought the whole place was awesome. He gasped, impressed to the power of thirty-three and a half!

'This, Tunde, is **The Complex**,' Professor Shapiro

said. 'As Professor Krauss has probably told you, we are going to be running tests on you and some other kids here. The tests shouldn't take long, but some of them will be hard. But the good thing to know is that you're all mostly at the same level – though I do believe you may have saved the world a couple of times more than most.'

Tunde looked a little sheepish, and felt himself blush.

The professor smiled at him and picked up something that looked like a necklace from a nearby desk.

'This is a simultaneous translator, something we've been working on here for the last few months – try it.'

She helped him fasten it around his neck and continued to explain.

'We wanted everyone to be able to communicate with each other.'

She pressed a button on the necklace and said something that sounded like: *'Wie hört sich das an, verstehst du mich?'*

But what Tunde heard was: 'How does this sound, do you understand me?'

Tunde was amazed – the translator device worked seamlessly. 'This is fantastic! You could absolutely flog this at Ruthvale market on a Sunday!'

Professor Shapiro grinned at his enthusiasm.

'Good.' She patted him on the shoulder. 'Now let's introduce you to some people. I think you're going to have a good time here, Tunde.'

Professor Shapiro continued to smile as the doors shut behind them and Tunde felt a **SINKING** feeling in his stomach, as if he were still descending in the lift.

3

Professor Shapiro led Tunde to what looked like a common room. It was a cavalcade of colour: brightly hued sofas and chairs, TV and gaming screens and a pile of the brightest, tastiest looking cakes Tunde had ever seen. There were bottles of FIZZY pop and also packs of chewy sweets. When Tunde grew up, he thought, he wanted a space just like this – but he'd probably add a water slide.

'It only gets better, Tunde,' Professor Shapiro said. 'Look at this.' She pressed a remote-control device that hung from her belt. Immediately, the ceiling divided and opened into four sections, revealing a large air space above. As Tunde looked up, he saw slalom sticks, multiple hoops, perches located in tricky positions, mini trampolines and large foam buffers placed everywhere just in case a power dive or swoop went awry and you found yourself **barrelling** towards the ground. Tunde stared at it all in wonder.

'An aerial practice space just for me? I can't believe it.'

'I thought I'd give you a bit of time to familiarize yourself with it before the tests begin. Do you want to have a go?'

Before she'd reached the word 'go', Tunde had tapped his chest three times to open up his wings and **rocketed** through the open ceiling and into the air space above.

'WOOOOOOOO HOOOOOOOOOO!'

He soared towards the slalom sticks and made short work of them, twisting in and out and through, like a winged cobra called Mr Twisty. Once he'd made it through them, he plummeted for a moment, then bounced off a mini trampoline.

'This is sick!' he yelled.

He jetted to the highest point he could reach, balanced on a convenient perch and looked all the way down at Professor Shapiro. From this vantage point, Tunde could see even more of **The Complex**. It seemed to be based on a box of tricks – there were numerous rooms with various bits and pieces of equipment that he couldn't quite make out from this height, but he saw activity in almost all of them. He power dived and landed on a lower perch and now he could see some of the people using the other rooms. What looked like a tree with long limbs, green soulful eyes and a full head of leaves was stretching, balancing and breathing loudly.

Suddenly, a voice in Tunde's head began to speak with an American accent: 'Her name is Klara-Phill. She's a kind of human-tree hybrid, from deep inside the Amazon rainforest. Klara's already a very powerful healer for someone so young – she's only about one hundred years old. I've said the odd word to her, but she doesn't say much back.' Tunde shook his head. It felt like someone had broken into his brain and

was running a pirate radio station from inside it. 'Er, excuse me, who are you? Could you get out of my head please? You shouldn't just hijack someone's brain and start talking to them without warning or asking if it's OK. That's basic etiquette.'

The voice was silent for a moment and then spoke again.

'Many apologies. Professor Shapiro thought it might be a fun way for me to introduce myself to you and also fill you in on some of the others. I absolutely should have asked your permission first. That was rude of me. They call me Headspayce – get it? I make space in your head for me. I can also hear what you're thinking.'

Tunde was concerned.

'Don't be concerned.'

'Wait, what? Stop! How do I stop you doing that?'

'Don't worry, I wouldn't do anything awful – although I did get into trouble at school cheating on exams; I just hijacked the answers for every question from the tutor's head. I could have been *Head* Teacher!'

Tunde laughed. But then he turned serious.

'What if I don't want you to read what's going on in my head?'

Headspayce replied, 'You'd have to be very clever and make me think of something else. But not many people can resist.'

Tunde pondered this before he asked his next question.

'You don't sound British, where are you from?'

'Minneapolis. Famous for the Twin Cities, lakes, Prince and, for some reason, an enormous rollercoaster near the airport.'

'That sounds boss. I've always wanted to ride on a luggage carousel, you know. Go round like one of the suitcases.'

Headspayce laughed, then stopped abruptly. '*Uh-oh*. You might want to buckle up.'

Someone came **rocketing** towards him! Before Tunde could think anything else, the flyer soared right past and jostled his shoulder, knocking him all the way across the room and into a well-placed foam mattress!

BLADDA-DADDA-BLA-FUMF!

The mattress absorbed the impact and, for a moment, Tunde felt safe. But then it b'doinged him out again.

The flyer was there, hovering, waiting for him. Tunde could see she was a girl and somehow had identical wings to his!

She crowed, 'Bet you thought you were special

when you came here? Well, not while I'm around. When I'm finished with you, you'll want to go flying back to your safe little nest.'

She took off and did the super slalom twice, then flew through some hoops – backwards, forwards and sideways! She performed commentary throughout.

'Oh, this is remarkable. Simul8 has only just borrowed these powers and is already showing more skill than the doofus she took them from. Here come the slalom sticks again. Let's try them upside down this time. Oh my word, that was sheer perfection! Let's try bouncing off the trampette, running along the wall one hundred metres up in the air, swinging from the parallel bars and then taking a selfie on one leg as I balance on the top perch.'

Tunde could feel Headspayce **FUMING** in his brain.

'I'm sorry, I should have warned you. She calls herself Simul8. Y'know, like simulate? She's from Germany and she can copy *anybody*. But, and don't tell her I know this, she can't steal someone's power forever. It takes a bunch of energy to even temporarily hijack a superpower, so there's a time limit. But she'd tell you her powers are boundless. Oh God, I hope she's not using **MY** powers to read my thoughts!'

As he said this, Simul8 flew backwards through the hoops with her hands over her eyes.

Tunde was furious. He took flight and proceeded to follow her. As Simul8 banked left, so did Tunde. When she dropped one hundred metres, Tunde followed. When she bounced off the ceiling, the wall, the trampoline, the **wobbly** perch, the floor and Professor Shapiro's pastry desk, Tunde did exactly the same and also, rather cheekily, grabbed a chocolate cupcake on the way. Simul8 tried to grab it from him, but Tunde had already gulped it down hungrily. He flew to the very top of the air space and hovered imperiously.

'I think I win, don't you? Get your own cake next time.'

Simul8 lowered herself to the ground and flounced off, shedding Tunde's powers at the same time. 'Flying's a stupid power anyway!' she yelled as her wings disappeared. And then she was gone.

'Hey, Tunde. It was nice to meet you. Sorry about trespassing in your brain. Maybe we could meet up in person soon and I can introduce myself properly with chocolate biscuits, rainbow chews and the first five editions of *United Powers*?'

Tunde yelped. '*United Powers?* I love that comic. I can't wait to meet you in person. I'll see if I can find some snacks and we can make it a fair trade.'

'Deal,' Headspayce said and then Tunde felt him leave his mind.

When Tunde returned to Shapiro's office, she was waiting for him, a curious smile playing on her lips.

'Well, that was intriguing, Mr Wilkinson. I saw you exploring **The Complex** and then playing with Simul8. She's a very interesting girl. Doesn't seem to be very concerned with teamwork.'

Tunde replied, 'My friend, Kylie, is always saying: "The ones that yell and kick and scream the most are the ones who need the biggest hugs." She drives us all mad. None of us wants to go around hugging bullies.'

Professor Shapiro looked at him carefully. 'And

what would you do if a bully was picking on you?'

Tunde thought for a moment.

'If I was at school, I'd tell a teacher, but if I was out, I'd run or try to get away, maybe talk to them. The last thing I'd want to do is fight . . . Though sometimes my dad says the only thing you can do is bonk a bully on the beezer.'

Professor Shapiro laughed.

'It says in my file that you fought off an alien invasion almost single-handedly. That you deactivated a robot that was about to destroy your house. That doesn't sound very much like running away or reasoning.'

Tunde shrugged. 'It turns out there are some times when my dad is right. Doesn't mean I have to enjoy it.'

Professor Shapiro nodded. This was going to be very interesting.

She showed Tunde to his bedroom and living area. He looked around in amazement at all the cool stuff in the room – a hot bath ready and waiting for him; warm milk and biscuits; furry white towels with his name embroidered onto them; and peanut butter and jam sandwiches under a glass dome should he need them before bedtime. Best of all, his closet was filled with super-suits just like the other kids had been wearing.

'Now, please hand over your phone. There's no reception down here anyway, but it's required because everything you see here is top secret. In the meantime, we meet for breakfast in the morning, exactly fifteen minutes after the alarm call. That should give you time to get ready. See you in the morning for the first round of tests.'

Tunde nodded, it all seemed fair enough to him. As he handed his phone over, he said, 'Can I use a landline to call Mum and Dad at the end of the day?'

Professor Shapiro shook her head. 'Tunde, we're here to work. Not to be on the phone to our parents all the time.'

Before he could reply, she was gone and he couldn't help thinking that something had changed in Professor Shapiro's voice just then.

Maybe he was hearing things. But his instinct told him otherwise.

4

Tunde woke up to the sound of church bells RINGING. He didn't remember falling asleep in a belfry. The bells DINGED and DONGED so loud he rushed to get ready just to escape from them. Despite hurrying he was still nearly late for breakfast. And what a breakfast it was!

Each person standing in the queue with crunchy, nutty cereals, or scooping doorstep-thick slices of toast and marmalade into their mouths, or piling their plate high with bacon, eggs, sausages and mushrooms was a **wonder**.

Tunde could see Klara-Phill, with her branch-like fingers dipped in a large bowl of green sludge which seemed to be reducing by the second. There was an extremely tall (no, honestly, REALLY TALL) brown girl with a shock of black, shaggy hair. She kept tripping over her shoelace. Tunde could see the problem. Every time she tripped, she became anxious and would grow twice her size, which meant her fingers were suddenly too big to retie her shoelaces. It looked as though all her clothes were specially

made to change shape with her, but the shoelace situation remained a problem.

Tunde rushed over and helped double-knot her super-thick shoelaces. 'There you go. All sorted.'

'Oh, thank you,' the girl said. 'My name's Yetie and I guess I'm not very good at controlling my power.'

She turned back to the breakfast buffet and as she did, Tunde saw her shoelaces undoing themselves again . . . !

'Wait!!' Tunde yelled, as Yetie CRASHED, painfully, to the floor.

He immediately heard Simul8 laughing and whipped his head around to find her eating cereal next to a shock-headed boy, who looked alarmed.

'I'm not doin' that to that lass,' he said in a northern accent. 'Who's doin' that?'

Simul8 cackled. 'Backflash here can go backwards in time by thirty seconds,' she explained to Tunde.

Tunde's eyes flashed angrily. Simul8 was using Backflash's powers to push back time and reverse Yetie's shoelace tying. And she was showing off.

'Why would you **do** that?'

'Because **it's funny,** Mr Goody-Goody, boy scout, help old ladies with shopping, rescue cats from up a tree, give goldfish mouth-to-mouth! You are literally Mr McBoring from Boringham.'

She marched off, cloned Yetie's powers briefly and enlarged herself to three times her actual size just to prove her point.

Just then, Tunde heard a familiar voice, 'Gosh, she really is annoying. She should have her own podcast, 'cause then we could switch her off!'

Tunde turned round to find a small kid wearing giant glasses standing next to him. He was rather weedy and had huge eyes due to the thickness of his lenses.

'I'm Headspayce. Don't worry, I know. I am so much **more** impressive in real life.'

Tunde laughed out loud.

'These are for you, as promised,' Headspayce said, as he handed over a pile of comics.

As they sat, ate and read comics over breakfast,

they got to know each other a bit better. With his mouth full, Headspayce asked, 'So, where are you from? I'm asking because I *don't* just want to shoplift it from your brain.'

Tunde then told him everything about Ruthvale, about the weird shop names, the healthy-eating cafe, *Tegan Regan's Vegan*, the mouse exterminator called *Squeaky Finders* and the new barbers *Ruthvale Hairport*.

Headspayce laughed. Tunde liked him.

'It's good to have someone here I can talk to,' Tunde said. 'I haven't been here very long and I want to know everything.'

Headspayce replied, 'Well, we've *all* only just arrived, but, let me get this straight, you wanna know everything? Are you sure? Like which toilets are blocked? When's the best day to avoid the canteen? Who has really stinky feet? *Everything* everything?'

Tunde laughed. 'You're funny. My dad's funny too – he's all about the jokes?'

'Ohh, what kind of jokes? Knock knock, one-liners, story jokes?'

'He likes all sorts. He'll just come up to me and say: "I had a horrible dream last night, Tunde – I dreamt I ate a massive marshmallow. I woke up this morning – the pillow was gone!" Or "I went to the doctors the other day. He said: I haven't seen you for a while. I said: I've been poorly." Or "I went to the corner shop the other day – bought four corners."'

Tunde had to stop because all he could hear in his mind was Headspayce's laughter. He was trying to think of more of his dad's 'best' jokes to share when Professor Shapiro's voice cut through the atmosphere like a white-hot knife through a pound of lard.

'Hello, students,' she **boomed** through the announcement system. 'Welcome to **The Complex** – we hope you're enjoying your breakfast. I highly recommend the iced twisty buns with raisins. The tests begin in ten minutes, so I suggest you do whatever you want: visit the bathroom, take another shower, comb your hair, clean your teeth, meditate. The alarm bells will tell you when it's time for the first test. Thank you.'

Tunde returned to his room and closed his eyes for a while. Kylie had shown him how to meditate. You sat still, breathed in for a count of ten and then out for ten and then if you simply listened to whatever was going on around you, both outside and inside the room, there was a chance you'd find yourself in a place of complete peace and calm.

As he sat there, trying not to think, Tunde realized that he'd almost forgotten that Nev, Jiah, Dembe and Kylie were at the Land of Adventures up the M1 near Notts. He'd actually begun to think *his* little adventure in this place with all these other superpowered kids was going to be much more fun. Though he felt a little guilty about that.

He emptied his mind some more and the meditation slowly became a nap (this happened sometimes). He was in a room, there were others there. The big girl, and the shock-headed boy (who Headspayce said was from Doncaster), and some of the others. The walls were closing in! No one knew what to do. Yetie held the ceiling up with her bare hands. There was screaming, and the ceiling moved relentlessly towards them and the walls continued to converge on them and his wings, which had been outstretched, were now pinned tighter and tighter to his body and everyone was cheek by jowl. Tunde couldn't inhale any more – it was only a matter of time before—

Suddenly, Professor Krauss's voice was yelling,

TUNDE, YOU'VE GOT TO GET OUT!

Tunde woke immediately. The bells were RINGING.

It was time for the first test.

5

Tunde followed everyone else as Professor Shapiro's silky tones rang out over the speakers: 'Could you all make your way to the Hexagonal Hall now? Thank you!'

Everyone headed towards a large, extremely cluttered six-sided room with doors along four of its sides. There were lamp stands, cupboards, bookshelves, sofas, potted plants, tables, ladders, chairs, filing cabinets – it was as if a living room had held its breath for far too long and then **EXPLODED.**

Professor Shapiro's voice rang out from speakers hoisted in all corners of the room, 'Your first test is simple: There are seven of you and six gold discs.

Locate them all. They are placed in and amongst the highest, lowest and hardest-to-reach places in the room. Do your best. Be creative. But, most importantly, find them!'

As Tunde scanned the room, he saw that Yetie's laces were once again undone and she'd almost tripped twice as she entered. Tunde grabbed Yetie's laces and tied them into a tight knot. Yetie looked all the way down (she was eighteen metres tall at the time) at the winged boy at her feet and yelled ਤੁਹਾਡਾ ਧੰਨਵਾਦ ਵਿੰਗ ਮੁੰਡੇ which Tunde heard as a loud: THANK YOU WING BOY, the force of which almost knocked him off his feet.

Headspayce immediately appeared in Tunde's head: 'These translators are hyper-cool right? You gotta love **The Complex** . . . they got all the cool tech.'

By the time Tunde regained his footing, he saw that everyone else was in a panic, yelling, getting in each other's way, ***pushing, shoving, jostling, hustling, sweating, bustling,*** doing everything

they could to figure
out where the gold
discs had been concealed.

Tunde flew directly upwards for a moment
and hovered overhead: he saw Backflash jumping in
the air, missing a gold ring, then going back in time
for thirty seconds, fetching a chair, climbing onto it
and then jumping at it again – and then missing it
again. Tunde swooped down and gave Backflash a
winged lift for the next try. Success!

63

He saw another kid create a mini-tornado, blowing everything around until a gold disc **bounced** across the floor.

One by one, the superkids found discs and were buzzed out of the game into the breakout room.

Klara-Phill, the tree creature, had simply extended her branches to search all corners of the room, but Tunde could see that she was missing areas where the discs might be located. He caught her eye and gestured that she might need some smaller twiglets to help. She found a gold disc in the bottom drawer of an overlarge filing cabinet and Tunde swooped down to give her the assist to pull it out.

As he helicoptered around the space, he saw a gold disc balanced on a shelf way above everyone's heads and out of reach near where Yetie was looking. He yelled at Yetie, 'Yetie, there's a disc there!'

And immediately Simul8 copied Yetie's powers and **ENLARGED** herself to reach for the disc. Luckily, Yetie beat her to the punch. Simul8 was furious and shrank back down in a right old huff. Tunde yelled out triumphantly. Mission complete!

And soon it was all over – Tunde was the last person flying around an empty room. As he landed and trudged into the breakout room, he suddenly realized no one had offered to help him and that he had been left without a single gold disc.

At the gaming table, Headspayce sat proudly gesturing at his gold disc. Tunde's spirits spiralled downwards, all his confidence disappearing with them. He wondered if he shouldn't just slink back to his room. And then he thought about how Dembe would leave. Based on the way she'd celebrate scoring a goal, he suspected that Dembe would exit with her head high, shoulders down, and then, just before she reached the door, pretend to comb her hair, brush imaginary dandruff from her shoulders, do a fast spin, point with two fingers – and only then strut out. So Tunde did exactly that . . .

And found himself in a broom cupboard.

As he re-entered the room laughing at himself, there was a loud **SZHEEEEB!** noise and then white-coated staff members wearing large goggles and carrying stopwatches and computer tablets appeared.

Professor Shapiro was slowly lowered down in a see-through lift shaft.

Headspayce's voice appeared in Tunde's brain: 'She *does* like to make a grand appearance, doesn't she?'

Tunde immediately stopped laughing as Professor Shapiro walked into the centre of the room, her face a mask of disappointment.

'Well, *that* was rubbish, wasn't it? A gold disc? This isn't Hogwarts! I was more interested in how you all worked together. Did anybody have any fun at all during the exercise?'

A lone tree branch raised itself into the air. Klara-Phill had a big grin on her face.

Professor Shapiro nodded. 'Thank you, Klara-Phill. Anybody else?'

Yetie raised her hand. 'I made a friend!' She then pointed at Tunde.

Professor Shapiro continued, 'Tunde Wilkinson was the only person in this room who tried to help others. The rest of you tripped over each other like comedy clowns in five-foot-long shoes to snaffle yourself a fake gold disc.'

Simul8 snorted her disapproval and glared at Tunde. 'At least I **got** a disc!'

Tunde was embarrassed. She was right. He might have helped everyone, but what did he have to show for it?

Immediately, though, Professor Shapiro leapt to his defence: 'The fact that you actually found a disc wasn't the real object of the game. Tunde Wilkinson led by example and helped his teammates, sacrificing his own chances of getting a gold disc. So, thanks to him, that means you **all** get the rest of the day off. More tests tomorrow, but for now, enjoy!' She smiled encouragingly at Tunde.

That was a game-changer. Everyone looked at each other – *Time off? YAAAAAAY!*

Simul8 glowered until you could almost see the steam pouring from her ears.

Tunde was in shock. He then grinned like a fox

who'd just discovered a chicken coop with its back door open. **The Complex** wasn't so bad after all, he thought to himself.

But all that was about to change.

All of the superkids sat in the leisure lounge, which had every kind of computer game you could think of, from the rubbishy old-school ones where two white squares pretended to bat another white square back and forth with a BING! and then a BONG!, to the frighteningly realistic Total Conquest of the Warrior Trolls, where the characters almost allowed you into the game with them to **zap, hack and slash** everything that moved within. There were brightly coloured bulbous seats, like giant inedible gobstoppers. There was a light-up BOOGIE BOUNCE DANCE-A-THON machine with neon squares that illuminated when the soles of your feet landed on them. Tunde and Headspayce had a great time busting moves (Tunde out-boogieing Headspayce – but only just). However, when Yetie challenged Klara-Phill, they became more and more excited as they got their respective grooves on and accidentally smashed the machine to *SMITHEREENS*. Afterwards, the whole thing looked as though it had been trampled by a herd of funk-tastic elephants.

This was the pattern of their time at **The Complex** – relaxing in the leisure lounge after a busy programme of tests. One day, they'd be set a crazed obstacle course where their feet weren't allowed to touch the ground, and then the next test would be all about water and holding their breaths. Sometimes there were complicated puzzles and other times it was all about Yetie's height, or Tunde's agility, or Simul8's ability to clone the powers of two or three or four people simultaneously, or Tai-phoon (that was the tornado-creating-kid. Turned out he could do lots of other cool stuff with weather too!) creating an ice slide to escape VR Zombies. Professor Shapiro was always watching and listening and making notes on her ever-present computer notepad. She set tasks that seemed impossible just to see what the superkids would do and how they'd cope. Despite their inexperience, they seemed to be performing quite well on the tests. And they were recovering from each strenuous session quicker and quicker.

After a few more days of this, the team had grown more comfortable with each other. They'd retire to the huge games room and chill out and chat.

It was on day ten when the big change happened.

Everyone sat around, drank milkshakes and ate snacks that resembled real food but were made entirely from chemicals – mmm, **delicious**. And they chatted in a way they hadn't before. They had stopped being shy and were able to talk about who they were in a relaxed manner.

Backflash, the boy with the shock of dark hair and a northern accent, was excited about the last test they had all just about completed. He had a big grin on his face. 'That were great that were. I've always liked competitions – but when I got me powers up home, I'd use 'em for stupid stuff – y'know – I'd get to the finish line at sports day and if I wasn't winning, I'd turn back time till I was. Me mum and dad saw me do it one day and grounded me for a fortnight, said I needed to learn about being honest. But to me it were just fun. But they made me see that using me powers to get me own way, y'know, to win, was wrong.'

Tunde was curious to know more. His powers also gave him an edge during sports days and football matches. 'So how *do* you stop yourself from using your powers to cheat?' he asked.

Backflash laughed. 'I've just got this picture of me mum and dad in me head. Me mum's got all me comics and me game consoles in a big bag and she's holding 'em over a fire. Me dad's just glarin' at me like he's gonna chew me head off. It's easy to do the right thing wi' that in yer head.'

Everyone laughed, even though Tunde couldn't quite tell if Backflash was being serious or not.

Tai-phoon spoke next. He was stocky and strong

and eager, had light brown skin and plaited long black hair. 'My mother and father are proud of me. I was chosen from eleven children to be here. We are a family of makers – some of us make canoes and houses, some make art and sculptures. I was the only one that made the weather.'

Tunde was impressed. 'You make the weather? I thought you could just control it?'

Tai-phoon laughed. 'I've always done it. When I was born, they say I cried for a week and made it rain until we were waist-deep in water. Mum held me in her arms day and night and sang to me until I eventually smiled. That's when the sun came out. The elders made Mum and Dad promise that when I was older, I would only use my powers for good and for our people.'

Everyone was enraptured by Tai-phoon's story.

Tunde looked at Klara-Phill and was wishing he could hear her story. But he wasn't sure he had ever properly heard her *talk*.

Then they all heard a symphonic, almost melodious voice, like a hundred accordions playing at the same time, in their heads, saying, 'Oh, I can talk, it's just that my voice would soon give you a headache. When we sing our songs in the rainforest, they are not for human ears.'

Everyone heard *that*. Tunde smiled and said, 'Is that

really where you're from then, the Amazon rainforest?'

Klara-Phill leaned her bushy head to one side. 'Oh yes. We are from what **you** call the Amazon but what **we** actually have named Mother. She holds, feeds and protects us. There are not many like me left. We are chosen.'

Tunde nodded. He had been dubbed the Son Foreseen by his birth mother and father, so he knew what that felt like.

Klara-Phill continued, 'We move beneath the cover of the canopy. For food or drink when our seedlings need sustenance. We bed down into the earth when we seek to be repaired. Mankind is a curse where I am from.'

Tunde had seen TV documentaries about what people had done in the rainforests, building, chopping down trees, ruining the climate.

Klara-Phill eyed Tunde. 'You understand a great deal about my home.' And then she twirled a branch-like tendril towards him and wrapped it around his arm in a hug.

'Why do you ask so many questions, bird-boy?' came a nasty voice from across the room. Simul8 borrowed Klara-Phill's power for a moment and became a tree person too – she wrapped a giant rubbery leaf around Tunde tightly, so tightly he couldn't move. 'Are you a spy? You trying to get all our secrets to use them against us in the tests?' she continued.

Yetie stood up and rumbled towards them, 'Stop! We were just talking.'

Tai-phoon looked at Tunde and Simul8 and, with a gesture, made it snow directly over their heads. He yelled, 'Pack it in now, Simul8. You're hurting him!'

Headspayce leapt onto Simul8's back, his thoughts bombarding her brain. 'Leave Tunde alone! Leave him alone! LEAVE HIM ALONE!'

Simul8 let go of Tunde and he sucked in air, a look of relief on his face. He could breathe again. He shook with cold.

And then came the near-silent **shzeeeeb!** of the doors opening – it was Professor Shapiro with an escort of guards.

'Everyone to your rooms NOW!' she demanded.

Everyone filed out sheepishly. They hadn't been brought here to fight each other. They were here to work together and improve their skills.

Tunde brought up the rear. He wasn't used to being the one that needed saving. He was shaken and wanted to hear familiar voices. He approached Professor Shapiro and asked as politely as he could, 'May I get my phone back for a moment to call my mum and dad, please.'

She looked at him, smiled sweetly and said, 'You want your phone back? After practically causing World War Six in here? The answer's no! Go to your room and when it's time – Go To Bed! You'll need all your energy in the morning.' Her smile turned into a grimace and she shooed him away with an imperious wave of her hand.

Tunde was miserable. He just wanted to call Mum and Dad! This wasn't fair. If he was stuck here for ages jumping through hoops, it's the least they could do! He thought, *If she won't give me my phone . . . I'm just gonna get it myself.*

He ran through what he might do to retrieve his phone. There were several options: he could just go to Professor Shapiro's office and take it. He wondered if he could get Yetie to grow super-sized and headbutt the wall surrounding Professor Shapiro's office? Maybe he could go nuclear and use his Blackfire powers to melt the entire building?

As Tunde's thoughts grew wilder and wilder, he heard Headspayce laughing in his mind.

'If you're about to sneak off and go snooping around,' his new friend said, 'then you're definitely going to need my help.'

7

Tunde and Headspayce sneaked out of their rooms and met in the hallway. Tunde loved watching films with his dad about mysterious secret agents and spies who fired laser beams and carried exploding suitcases and radioactive compasses. Now it felt like he was in one of those movies.

Headspayce beamed his thoughts directly into Tunde's head. 'You're right to ask questions. She's taken all our phones and no one's been able to call anyone. She always says no.'

Tunde fumed, 'Well, let's do something about that. We're gonna get everybody's phones. Not letting us talk to our families is very fishy . . .'

They tiptoed quickly down a side corridor and stopped for a moment. There was a security guard the size of a small building standing by one of the sliding doors. He wore white overalls, carried a computer tablet and had a grubby security card hanging from his belt. Headspayce approached him before Tunde could say, 'WHAT ARE YOU DOING? GET BACK HERE!'

The security guard looked at Headspayce beadily. 'Er, what you doin' round here?'

Headspayce was as cool as a cucumber on a skiing holiday. He met the guard's beady stare without flinching and just said, 'I was invited here – wasn't I?'

The guard blinked several times and stared into Headspayce's eyes. 'I think that's right. You were invited here. Absolutely.'

Headspayce stared at him, unblinking. 'And I was told that all I had to do when I got to this part of the building was ask for . . .' And he read the guard's name tag, 'Wolfgang – that's you, isn't it?'

Wolfgang the guard stood to attention proudly. 'I am Wolfgang, yes. I am – Wolfgang. No doubt about it.'

Headspayce beckoned to Tunde, who came out into the open and watched this entire pantomime play out. He winked at Tunde and continued speaking quietly to the now mesmerized guard. 'So, Wolfgang, you need to take that card from your belt and hand it over to us and then you probably need to dance a little jig for half an hour, would you do that for me?'

Wolfgang handed Headspayce his security card, complete with bungee cord, and then proceeded to dance a sailor's hornpipe-type dance whilst humming, 'What shall we do with the drunken sailor' **over** and **over** and **over** again.

Tunde couldn't have been more shocked. 'That was, like, Jedi-level, Headspayce. Bruv, how did you do that?'

Headspayce led the way and explained as they searched for the door to Professor Shapiro's office. 'Turns out, part of putting my voice in people's heads is making them think my voice is their thoughts! So I can suggest things and make them think it was their own idea!'

Tunde almost broke out into a cheer. 'That's brilliant, we might have to use that if we need to get out of here—'

Headspayce looked at him and shook his head. 'Uh, no, Tunde, it only works on really stupid people – Professor Shapiro would see through that in a heartbeat.'

Headspayce adopted a secret-agent-type pose as they tiptoed down the corridor.

Tunde couldn't help but laugh as he did the same, **DUCKING** and **WEAVING** around corners. He realized that perhaps he'd become too used to having adventures. Once you'd saved the world once or twice, you kind of got used to it. This was Headspayce's first time and he was enjoying every second.

They used the card to pass through three no-go areas. There were lots of increasingly larger Keep Out signs in bright red luminous paint. 'STOP' and 'I've told you once' and 'Can't you read you big numpty?'.

Headspayce pointed, 'I'm starting to think . . . they don't want us to be here.'

They both cracked up at this, but then had to quickly stop themselves as a golf buggy with four guards **SHUZZZED** nearer and nearer. **They were going to be caught!**

In an instant, Tunde grabbed his friend, extended his wings quickly and, with two beats, flew up to the ceiling and waited till they'd driven by. Tunde gently floated back down to ground level.

Headspayce shook himself and said, 'Next time you do that, d'you mind if I fasten my seat belt first! Never even got my peanuts.'

They came to a nearby utility ladder. Tunde climbed up it and gestured for Headspayce to do the same. There was a large vent over their heads and lots of steel piping.

'We should crawl through here and see if there's a way into Professor Shapiro's office. That's where she keeps everyone's phones. Come on.'

With imaginary action movie music playing in his head – or was that just Headspayce doing more mind tricks? – Tunde continued the snoop-a-thon! He crawled along the metal vent, with Headspayce following close behind and soon – having quickly swerved when they spotted two large rats with glowing eyes fighting over a mouldy cheese and pickle sandwich – they found themselves directly above Professor Shapiro's tower office. They heard her talking on the phone – it sounded serious – she was getting more and more angry as she spoke.

'Of **course** it's going to work. Because I'm **me** that's why. I've done the research – we isolate specific cells, freeze them until they don't work any more and then, **boom**, they're shut down like Disneyland during the pandemic! Once we've frozen their DNA then we can easily reproduce—'

And then, because he was stuck in a confined space and couldn't move and also because of all the dust floating around, and *also* also because Headspayce kept sniffing and wiping his nose, Tunde let loose the sneeze of all sneezes – ACHOOOOOOO!

As the thunderous sneeze rang out, Tunde's wings shot out into full extension in the confined space, knocking Headspayce flat on his face. **SPANG! CLANG! B'DANG!**

The whole pipe broke away from the ceiling and wobbled loose. Tunde and Headspayce fell from the

broken pipe like candy from a piñata!

WHAM! BAM! BUDUMP!

They landed smack bang in the middle of Professor

Shapiro's observation room.

Suddenly, there were guards everywhere, all holding long metallic electrified sticks. They were completely surrounded.

8

Professor Shapiro waited, arms folded. 'Well?'

There was a silence. Even though they were thousands of metres below ground, Tunde swore he could hear crickets.

And then Headspayce said, 'Um, Professor Shapiro, we've been enjoying the tests so much, we wondered if there were any more golden discs that hadn't been found. So we had a good old look in the pipes!'

Tunde looked at Headspayce as if he were mad, but then nodded vigorously. He added, 'Yes, and, um, Professor Shapiro, I was also wondering if I could call my mum and dad. I'm homesick. I just wanted to make one teeeeeny call.'

And he smiled nervously like a tiny mouse grinning at a full-sized lion in a bid for mercy.

Professor Shapiro took off her glasses and looked at the pair closely. She smiled at them, then opened a drawer in her desk, producing Tunde's phone from within. 'You know – if I believed any of that nonsense you just said, my life would be much easier. I could send you back to your room and you could get a shower and prepare for tomorrow's tests and everything would be peachy and groovy and we'd all be friends again. But NO. You had to go snooping around making your little jokes and *eavesdropping* on people.'

She pressed a button on a remote control and suddenly Tunde saw himself and Headspayce on a number of screens dotted around the place – creeping through the pipes, staring through the vents, encountering the large glowy-eyed mutant rats and then freaking out. Their every move had been recorded.

Tunde's next few words came out in a torrent.

'Look, we're both sorry, we shouldn't have done it! Just kick us out and we'll go home and won't say any more about it!'

Professor Shapiro made a signal with her hand which meant 'zip it, now'.

Tunde quietened and Headspayce filled the silence. 'Tunde, we're not going home any time soon. The Prof's got big plans for us and it's all about our powers and what she can do with them. She's a power leech.'

Professor Shapiro looked tired. 'Quiet, Norman, you're annoying me.'

Tunde looked at Headspayce. 'Norman?'

'I don't wanna talk about it. My parents need major therapy – and after this, after what Professor Shapiro does to us . . . so will I.'

Tunde didn't know what he was talking about. Headspayce filled him in.

'No way is she gonna let **any** of us go, so you can forget that. She just wants to leech our powers and then sell them to the highest bidder!'

Professor Shapiro nodded. 'Correct-a-mundo,

Norman – it's almost like you read my mind. Note to self – increase mental shields in the presence of nosey-parker telepaths. But first . . .' She signalled to the biggest of the guards, who grabbed Headspayce from behind and hoisted him onto his shoulder.

Tunde yelled, 'Headspayce! Make him put you down and do the Funky Chicken.'

Headspayce furrowed his brow until his forehead resembled a mutant prune, but nothing happened. 'It's no good. He's too smart. We're toast!'

'Well, that was **very** entertaining – scrunching your face like that – you should be on TV.' Professor Shapiro yelled at her security guards, 'Take him away and get him prepped for a full DNA extraction. This has been enough messing about. His powers WILL be mine.'

'**NOOO!**' Tunde yelled and then extended his wings and rose from the ground, preparing to fly at Professor Shapiro. He had no idea what he would do when he got to her, but he knew she **had** to be stopped.

But Shapiro wasn't the least bit bothered by Tunde

suddenly taking flight. She merely picked up a shiny remote device, clicked a button and his wings simply vanished. He dropped to the ground with a **THUD.** His powers weren't working! Professor Shapiro barked a laugh like a Labrador watching a penguin falling off a skateboard on YouTube.

'Now, *that* is impressive. Look at you. You're a little flightless humanoid brat now, aren't you? You are fascinating. You were so easy, Tunde. One of the

most powerful kids here and yet you have no idea what you can do.' She continued, spitefully – 'And the thing is, without your powers you're just an average, little boy with no ambition. You depend on everyone around you – your parents, your beloved friends. Ever since you've been here, Yetie, Headspayce and Taiphoon have all helped you. You're like a damsel in distress – but there's no one here to rescue you now. I'm going to STEAL your powers too – then the world will finally see what Abigail Shapiro can really do!'

9

Now, you may or may not have noticed that Tunde's phone was on Professor Shapiro's desk during all of this COMMOTION. This was no mere shop-bought phone. Oh no, gentle reader. This was a phone designed by Professor Emil Krauss, Chief Executive and guiding light of **The Facility**.

The Facility produced many different types of things – they didn't just investigate parallel dimensions and work with mutated animals and vegetables and artificial intelligence. They also invented super-cool gadgets and gizmos too.

Tunde wasn't allowed to have a mobile phone for a long time. He wasn't a fully fledged teenager yet and his mum and dad figured he could wait a while before having access to EVERY SINGLE THING in the world via the click of a button. They thought that, perhaps, he needed to concentrate on school, homework, sports and keeping the carpet in his bedroom Y-front free. Being able to watch clips from every *Cave Fighter Extreme* movie or snippets from *Bake Me Something Bizarre* should not be at the top of his priority list.

But, eventually, as all parents do, they gave in. Once he had discovered his wings, the Blackfire powers and his position as EARTH AND RUTHVALE'S FIRST LINE OF DEFENCE against aliens from within and without, they thought having a phone might be a good way for him to stay in touch and tell them if he was going to be late for his tea because he was battling with a Fungoid Blob Monster by the petrol station up town.

Up until now, however, Tunde had only ever called his mum to say he would be late for his tea due to working on homework at school so 'Don't bother cooking the beetroot and mustard with an almond crust pie for me just now' or 'It's a game tonight, Mum, so do you mind if I get fish and chips on the way home with Nev? No, he doesn't want a shrimp trifle with jackfruit custard. He says he'd eat it all and there'd be none for no one else. No, you can't hear someone pretending to be sick in the background. It's just Nev clearing his throat'.

But being made by **The Facility,** Tunde's phone had many uses besides making and receiving calls. It also monitored his body temperature and anxiety levels; it could read the airspace around him like air traffic control at Heathrow and sense the heat signatures of any dangerous-looking creature in a forty-five-mile radius. It had a GPS tracking system that made James Bond's look like a scrunchy paper map. However, the best thing about Tunde's phone – or the *Fac-One* as Professor Krauss called it – was that it was voice-controlled.

Remembering this, Tunde yelled at the top of his voice: 'FAC-ONE, call Artie – I'm in real danger!'

On Professor Shapiro's desk, his phone immediately vibrated and patched him in. It spoke: 'YOU MAY BEGIN, TUNDE!'

Tunde didn't need an invitation, 'ARTIE, ARE YOU THERE?'

'Tunde what do you need? Your heart rate's going nuts, your blood sugar's OK, but you need to drink at least two litres of water. You're as dry as Death Valley High Street in the summer holidays. Are you OK?'

'No. None of us are. It's a trick! Professor Shapiro wants to steal everybody's powers.'

And the next voice he heard was Krauss's – 'Tunde – Artie patched me through – are you all right?'

'No. Professor Shapiro's batty as a Batcave full of batty bats – she wants to steal our powers from us – it's just a way to make money or destroy the world – you've got to—'

Professor Shapiro laughed sweetly. Putting on a sweet, soothing voice like when Beyoncé sings the mushy, quiet love songs, she spoke over Tunde addressing Professor Krauss, but a guard had covered Tunde's mouth with his hand so he couldn't make a sound anyway.

'Professor Krauss, what a lovely surprise! We're just having lots of fun here after a day of brilliant experiments. The kids are relaxing, playing some of our state-of-the-art games, but little Tunde here – ever the prankster – thought it would be funny to make some prank calls! Boys will be boys, I suppose.'

Tunde could hear Professor Krauss LAUGHING. He tried to speak, but he couldn't.

Professor Krauss replied. 'Actually, I wanted to pick your brains about an issue we're having with the magnetopause of the interplanetary space beyond Saturn, and this problem I came across when looking at the spaghettification of supergiants by gravitational tidal forces but those sound like tomorrow problems! Have a great night, goodbye.'

Professor Shapiro hung up – reached into her desk and produced a large hammer and bashed Tunde's phone repeatedly with it.

BAM! WHAM! BADAM! PAM! GAM! SHAM! WHAMMO! KERSLAMMO!

The phone was completely destroyed.

Professor Shapiro stared at Tunde intently. 'Looks like you'll have to get an upgrade.'

Tunde was furious but, mad as he was, he also slowly felt his powers returning – Professor Shapiro's Power Leech gadget must have been wearing off! He tried to act like nothing was happening to avoid suspicion. He took a deep breath, trying to calm himself down like Kylie would suggest. He tried to think clearly, like Jiah would advise. And he needed to do something brave and fast, like Dembe or Nev.

See, Tunde had one more trick up his sleeve. As well as his ability to fly, he still had his special Blackfire power. And that could cause **a lot** of damage.

'I don't *want* to do this, Professor Shapiro, but you don't leave me any *choice!*'

The guard holding Tunde back laughed. But his smile soon disappeared when Tunde let loose the black flame, hitting the desk in front of him, and spread his wings in one smooth motion. He launched himself up into the air and flew above everyone's heads to **CRASH** through the windows of Professor Shapiro's observatory. Flying hundreds of metres above the ground, he turned to look back at her. But she wasn't distressed at all. In fact, she was grinning.

And Tunde soon understood why.

Professor Shapiro was holding the Power Leech remote and speaking as though she were addressing an adoring audience. 'Who is The Boy with Wings

without his wings?' she said. 'Just a boy?'

She pressed the button. And Tunde fell from a great height like an anvil with a giant boulder balanced on top of it.

It turns out there's a very thin line between flying and falling. Tunde was used to the feeling of air rushing past him as he swooped down, but now he was utterly helpless. Falling like this meant only one thing – landing **very hard** on the ground. As he continued to fall, he closed his eyes and he muttered a prayer which went something like:

'I promise I promise I promise not to take my wings for granted and to always be kind and not cheek my mum and dad and always do my homework on time. And, also, remember when I said Quinn Patterson totally has dung for brains and plays football like he has a stone in his boot and doesn't know anything about ANYTHING? I take it back.'

But then he felt something move around him. It was a gust of wind. It pushed him up and then sideways a little as he plummeted, slowing him down. The feeling continued and soon Tunde, falling more slowly, was surrounded by thick billowy clouds which were helping to cushion his fall. He slowed down so much that Yetie was able to gently pluck him out of the air, and set him safely down on the ground. Somehow he'd survived. And he had Tai-phoon and Yetie to thank for that. All the other superkids gathered around him in one of the testing rooms.

'Thank you – you saved my life.'

'You don't mention the wind. Whenever I use my wind-power nobody even wants to mention it. "Your wind saved my life!" Why won't people say that?'

Tunde laughed. 'I'm sorry. Your wind did save my life. Thank you.'

'His *wind* saved your life,' Simul8 snarked. 'You were saved by a giant *fart*. That's hilarious!'

The speaker system crackled and Professor

112

Shapiro's voice rang out loud and clear.

'Everyone pay attention and listen to me! This is important. Tunde Wilkinson has basically tried to ruin everyone's time here at **The Complex!** After all the things we've done – testing you, making sure you're fit for your futures, feeding you, giving you cool costumes and ice cream and movies, Mr Wilkinson thinks it's just fine and dandy to sneak around like a meddling busybody and steal from me! Well, we're in total lockdown now. No more treats or nice surprises for anyone! We'll continue the tests as before, but as soon as they're done, you'll be confined to your rooms until further notice. You'll be under surveillance twenty-four hours a day and your powers won't work until I want them to. You can be heroes. But only if you obey orders and behave like good little boys and girls. DO. YOU. UNDER. STAND. ME?'

The speakers wobbled and shook as she yelled. Everybody there – even members of staff in their pristine white coats, carrying their computer tablets dutifully – tried not to look frightened.

Headspayce, who'd just been bundled back into the room having had more blood taken and DNA tested, just decided to **be frightened.** Professor Shapiro added: 'Say YES, PROFESSOR SHAPIRO – WE UNDERSTAND!'

And the whole gathering of superkids felt their powers switch off and obeyed.

'YES, PROFESSOR SHAPIRO – WE UNDERSTAND!'

They were shepherded into a large room that seemed to have no ceiling. When Tunde looked up, the walls went on and on – higher than he'd ever seen Yetie grow even when she had her powers. Simul8 tried to open a nearby door. No luck. It was locked. Tai-phoon, Yetie and Backflash all had a go at jiggling the handles, squinting through keyholes, even running, jumping and hammering at doors. It was no good. The door was locked tightly shut. Whatever Professor Shapiro was planning next, it had to take place in this room.

Tunde was miserable. All he wanted was to go

to the best adventure play park this side of the M1 and now he was in this rotten **Complex** place, **and** he and all his new friends (plus Simul8) might lose their powers for good as a result.

Tai-phoon was watching him closely. He asked, 'What do you think we should do, Tunde?'

Simul8 couldn't believe her ears. 'What are you talking to him for? He's the reason we're all stuck here in the first place. What were you thinking, disobeying Professor Shapiro like that?'

Tunde could feel tears welling up in his eyes. 'I just wanted to call my mum and dad, or my mates. I want to go home.'

It was the worst he'd felt for ages. He hid his face as massive tears ran down his cheeks.

Simul8 screamed at him – 'BUT YOUR POWERS ARE KAPUT, YOU NUMBSKULL! ALL OUR POWERS ARE GONE! SEE?' And she clenched her fists and tried to summon her powers and copy *anyone's* powers, but she couldn't . . . nothing happened. She remained herself, just a kid with nothing supernaturally special about her at all. She burst into tears.

Backflash stuck his hand up, 'If my powers were workin', I could send us back in time and this wouldn't have happened yet.'

Everyone looked at him expectantly.

He continued. 'But I only go backwards in time for thirty seconds, so it wouldn't be enough. And I can feel it as well – me powers have gone. I'm gutted.'

At that, everyone began to moan and grumble and get a bit snuffly.

Tunde looked at his new friends. They might not be super special any more, but they were still some of the most extraordinary people he'd ever met. He tried to remember something that Kylie had said about trying to get people to listen. It was something to do with storytelling.

'We can get out of this,' Tunde said. 'Look at us – when I first came here, I didn't know anybody – I had no idea what you could do – I mean, you've seen what I can do – I can fly. But there's Simul8 who can copy anyone; Klara-Phill – she's literally a tree with a face; Yetie – she can grow; Tai-phoon controls the weather; Backflash can go back in time.'

'Yeah, but only for thirty seconds. Not much pigging use at all really.'

Tunde ignored him and continued. 'Right now, our powers are gone, but there must be *something* we can do to get out of this? Headspayce – you must have loads of ideas! Simul8 – you're good at being . . . well, you copy people, so you're used to thinking of lots of different solutions. Klara-Phill's been alive longer than everybody – you must have knowledge?' Tunde was trying to motivate everyone – including himself! – out of the slump. 'I know we're not even proper teenagers yet, but we have ideas, we can get out of this.'

Simul8 interrupted him abruptly – 'Human pyramid!'

Tai-phoon scoffed. 'That's just silly. It's too high!'

Backflash laughed 'Yeah, how we gonna get all the way up there?'

Simul8 opened her mouth to speak, but,

uncharacteristically, didn't say anything.

Tunde suddenly had a flash of his adopted sister Dembe, who was the most confident kid he knew and who had *still* needed the Wilkinsons, who were so used to chatting and joking amongst themselves, to make space for her when she'd moved in. He stepped forward. 'Hang on. Simul8, can you explain what you mean? Human pyramid like at the football after we've scored a goal and we all climb on top of each other?'

Simul8 screwed up her courage to speak again. 'Not like that. We work together to form a human pyramid – I climb to the top – jump down to the other side, find a pass key and let everyone out through the door.'

Tunde thought about it, then looked around at the others. Backflash wasn't sure, Headspayce was just standing there scrunching his face, frustrated that his powers weren't working right now. Klara-Phill seemed to be staring into space, not thinking about anything.

Tunde addressed the group, 'It's not a completely

terrible idea.'

'Yes! It's not a terrible idea at all!' Simul8 came back to her old self now that she had someone on her side. 'We'll live to fight another day – my name will be all over social media! I will be **famous!**'

Klara-Phill *hmmphed* several times, sounding like a German oompah band warming up before a show. 'It could work, but we need someone small at the top. Like Headspayce. We get him up there – *he* climbs over and down, *he* finds the key and comes back.'

The colour immediately left Headspayce's face. Everyone looked up at the huge walls hemming them in. It seemed like a daunting task building a human pyramid that high and if they managed, what then? There were no guards in this room now but what if they came back?

Tunde stared up into space, thinking, and then he had an **IDEA.**

'Look, I should do it . . . it should be me.'

Simul8 huffed and puffed.

Tunde ignored her. 'It's Simul8's plan but . . . I'm

not scared of heights, I'm used to being up there. If someone can get me up there – I'll find a way down. Trust me.'

Klara-Phill nodded her leafy head. 'This makes sense. Flying boy must be at the top. He will find a way down.'

Backflash agreed. 'She's right. Tunde should be at the top. Look at him, he can't wait to get up there – it's what he's used to.'

Tai-phoon nodded.

Simul8 rolled her eyes. 'I can fly too, y'know.'

'Yes, we do know,' Tai-phoon said, more gently than he would have before. 'But that's only when you hijack someone else's powers. Tunde was born to do this.'

'Can we just get on with it please – they're probably listening to this even as we speak!' Headspayce squeaked.

And that's how they all agreed to put Tunde at the top of the human pyramid.

11

A feat of amazing ingenuity began as everyone clambered over everyone else to create the **biᴢᴀrrest** superhuman pyramid anyone had ever seen, made up of shape-changers, growers, humanoid plants, limited time travellers, brainboxes and weather warlocks.

With Yetie at the centre of it all and Klara-Phill by her side, Backflash climbed onto Yetie's shoulders, Tai-phoon jumped up onto Klara, Headspayce found a space on Yetie's shoulder – and, before you knew it, Simul8 had given a leg-up to Tunde, who was now balanced PRECARIOUSLY at the very top like an awkward Christmas tree ornament.

Simul8 looked up at Tunde, who wavered and wobbled at the top of the wall.

'Hurry up!' she muttered angrily and then she boosted Tunde.

He fell backwards, surprised as he lost his balance.

This was something he wasn't used to doing. He **TUMBLED** over the wall and no one could help him. There was no timely gust of wind, no giant hand to catch him, no human plant creature to scoop him up. He just **PLUMMETED** hard, but as he did so, he spotted loops of pipes and speaker units and observation cameras dotted all the way down.

BAM! He grabbed a coil of pipe!

WHAM! His hand reached for an outward-jutting speaker unit, which smashed off as he hit it, but no matter, his fall had slowed for a moment.

And then **THUNK** – his shoulder smacked against a CCTV camera, but, quick as a flash, he grabbed at it for the briefest of moments and then he landed awkwardly with a **THUMP!**

Simul8 didn't even cast a look over her shoulder – she was over the wall in an instant and copying Tunde's fall exactly, moving with great speed and agility.

BAM! She landed on her feet, bent her knees a little and said: 'Whoa!'

Tunde looked gobsmacked. 'That was amazing. Are you all right?'

Simul8 stretched, her bones clicking and clacking into place, before saying, 'I'm fine. I copied what you did, but I improved on it a little. It's what I do – add a little **pizzazz!**' She paused for a moment and then added, 'You were quite brave, though. Well done.'

And then she ran off to find a pass key.

Tunde stayed on the lookout and was relieved when Simul8 reappeared. But only for a second . . .

'Get back up the wall,' she yelled.

Tunde could hear the heavy clatter of footsteps behind her.

They both scrambled up the wall, seeking out familiar handholds, and clambered up to the top in a matter of moments. They landed at the apex of the human pyramid and climbed back to the ground. Everyone gathered around as Simul8 produced the pass key and waved it in the air carelessly.

'Who needs powers?' she bragged.

'Not you,' retorted Backflash. 'As long as the goal

is to get the whole pigging **Complex** after us!'

Tunde was thinking. They had a key to get out of THIS room, but they were effectively surrounded and still stuck way, way underground. 'What we need now is a distraction,' he said.

Everyone looked at him.

Tunde continued, 'I'm in the football team. My mate, Nev, is our top goal scorer. He makes us do this thing where we distract our opponents so he can just ease into the penalty area and score. We need something like that.'

Simul8 pulled a face, but Klara-Phill tapped Tunde on the shoulder with her twiggy fingers and grinned.

MEANWHILE, outside, Professor Shapiro's security team were gathered, waiting for orders. A tall bloke in an ill-fitting uniform spoke for everyone as he whispered to the guard next to him, 'I didn't sign up for this. I thought I was doing lab work. Turns out, Shapiro wants us to grab any kid who gets out of line and chuck 'em in the bin!'

His colleague agreed, 'Yeah, I was s'posed to be doin' blood tests and DNA swabs. Instead, I'm here stopping superpowered kids from running away. I think Shapiro's as nutty as squirrel poo.'

The tall one laughed. 'Don't let her hear you say that. She'll tie your legs in knots, cover you in honey and shove an anthill—'

But he stopped talking. There was an insistent banging from the other side of the door and the sound of someone being very *poorly* indeed . . .

Tunde yelled, 'Hello? HELLO? Somebody please help. We've got a really sick person here. It's horrible.'

In the background, the guards listened and could hear noises like **HEUGGGGHHIEEE** and **BEUCLEUCH,** not to mention **DUGURRRRRRRRRRGH!**

The guards gingerly opened the doors and found Tunde holding on to Klara-Phill, who was bent double and surrounded by gallons of green . . . stuff.

Tunde looked sympathetic, appealing to their better nature. 'We've got to get her to the sickbay. There's obviously something wrong. Professor Shapiro needs to look at her as soon as possible.'

There were at least a dozen guards gathered in the doorway looking aghast at the horrific, green, gloopy mess.

The tall one moved towards Klara-Phill and Tunde with an outstretched hand. 'I think you're right. This is a complete m—'

But, before he could complete his sentence, Klara-Phill opened her mouth and SPEWED an unending thunderous AVALANCHE of green barf, which forcefully BLASTED the guards off their feet, sliding them away in a wash of disgusting-smelling chunder.

They all ran, with Tunde and Klara-Phill at the front, towards what they thought was freedom. They used one of the guard's pass keys to get into the next room and shut the door behind them as the greenified, gooified guards slipped and slid and slithered around miserably, trying and failing to stand up once more.

'This is DISGUSTING,' one of them groaned.

'What is that smell?' another one moaned.

'I'm never going to eat vegetables again.'

'I think *I'm* going to throw up now.'

'Oh no. Don't, 'cause if you do, I—
BUUUUIIIHICKGGGGHCKKK!'

12

Tunde and the other superkids were in a blue room. It was considerably different from where they'd just been. This space had a definite ceiling and lower walls. The floor sloped down at an angle. Everyone found it difficult to stay at the top near the door. They all slid down to the bottom and gathered there in a SOGGY LUMP. There were markings on the wall – horizontal dashes with numbers interrupting them.

Tai-phoon recognized where he was straightaway. 'This is where they tested all my weather powers.'

Tunde noticed that water was slowly starting to seep in and was now at his ankles and then, moments later, up to his calves. 'So how long did it take you to get out of here?'

The water was up to Tunde's shins now. He tried to remain calm.

Tai-phoon responded, chattily, 'Well, I can create weather, like a storm or a flood or anything, but I can also use the elements. I just iced everything and stepped out of here. As you British say, easy-peasy pudding and pie.'

Yetie pointed out the obvious, as the water reached Tunde's knees. 'But your powers are KAPUT now. No easy. No peasy. No pudding. No pie.'

The water was at waist-height now. Backflash was floating on his back.

'My powers have gone,' Tai-phoon said, defeatedly. He began to kick with his legs to stay afloat.

Panic was setting in. The water was chest-height already.

'Well, we've got to do something, this water's rising non-stop. It's only a matter of time before it's over our heads. And then it's sink or swim time.'

Almost everyone at this point was back-floating or

treading water. But then Tunde could hear yelling. Simul8 was screaming at Headspayce: 'You get water on my hair and I'll slap you silly! I will. ANYBODY splashes me and and and and and, I'll BITE THEM!! I mean it.'

And then she kicked and **splashed** a great deal and then sank again.

Everyone watched with great interest. No one swam over to help her. And then Tunde realized something.

OH NO . . .

Simul8 can't flipping swim!

He surged across to her, watching as she barely managed to stay afloat.

'Simul8,' he called. 'Can you swim?'

'Of course I never learned to swim,' she yelled. 'All I had to do was copy people, fish or ducks. Anything that could swim and then I could do it. Nobody ever expects to be in a room filling up with water until it's over your head. I'm going to look like a drowned rat. I don't even like water. IT'S WET!'

She sank again. Tunde dragged her back to the surface, but she fought him.

'Get off – glub. No, no! Blub— Urgh.'

The room was basically a giant aquarium now, the water creeping closer and ever closer to the ceiling. Everyone was SUSPENDED many metres above the ground, legs kicking, arms thrashing, trying to stay at the surface.

Tai-phoon swam towards Tunde wanting to talk,

but Tunde was busy calming Simul8 down.

'Kylie says the best way to calm down is to close your eyes, breathe in for five and out for five, and basically listen.'

Simul8 looked angry, but Tunde carried on regardless.

'Yeah, Kylie says you breathe in for 5, 4, 3, 2, 1 and you breathe out for 5, 4, 3, 2, 1.'

The water was continuing to rise, but, thankfully, Simul8 had begun to calm down. Because of her breathing and listening, she had dropped from level **Aaaaaargh!** down to level **Aargh!** She held on to Tunde's hand firmly and carried on breathing in and out – doing it almost for herself rather than for Tunde. In the meantime, Tai-phoon was at Tunde's shoulder.

'There's a big button near a closed drain right at the bottom. Maybe it opens the drain?'

'That makes sense. You wanna give it a go?'

Tai-phoon looked a bit nervous.

'That's a thirty-metre free dive with no air supply. I haven't got gills!'

'Tai-phoon, this is hero time. You can do this!'

Tai-phoon looked at Tunde and gave him a tight smile, and then **hurtled** towards the bottom of the room with powerful strokes.

Despite Simul8's breathing, she kept dipping under the water and Tunde had to keep dragging her back to the surface. He wasn't sure how much longer he could keep them both afloat.

There was little more than a metre of air space

above their heads now. Pretty soon, the entire room would be SUBMERGED. And then after that . . .

Tunde couldn't bear to think about it.

He yelled, 'Everybody, take big gulping breaths. Keep breathing as deeply as you can.'

And now there was just thirty centimetres of space left.

Yetie was panicking – 'I don't like this. I don't like this at all. AT ALL!'

She began pounding at the wall, to no effect.

Backflash was crying like a baby from Doncaster, 'If I had me powers, I could reset us to thirty seconds ago and we might have stood a chance.'

There was only ten centimetres of air left above the RISING water.

Tunde yelled at the top of his voice: 'Keep taking long pulls of air – we can do this.'

Now the water was only a few centimetres from the ceiling. There were moans and groans and the sound of prayers being said. This was it. Tunde saw what felt like a supercharged high-speed movie trailer of his life;

from hatching, to walking, to flying, to space travel, to unleashing Blackfire powers, taking down a cat alien and dismantling a giant robot. And then Nev, Jiah, Kylie, Dembe, Artie, Mum and Dad. Everyone and everything **ker-whooshed** past his eyes. This was *just like* his super-scary drowning dream. He realized, at that moment, that all he wanted to do was to help make everything all right if he could, with or without powers. People like Professor Shapiro shouldn't be allowed to treat anyone like this, whether they've got wings, or they can change shape, or grow to the size of Nelson's Column, or turn invisible—

SUDDENLY, a whirlpool appeared in the middle of the room and everyone began to spin, like an underwater tornado and the water level fell, first by a metre, then ten metres, then twenty metres until it was completely gone. They all came ***crashing*** to the floor.

Tai-phoon lay unconscious next to the drainage button.

'We need to help him!'

Simul8 ran across and started pounding on Tai-phoon's chest. Then, tilting his head just so and pinching his nose closed, she placed her lips directly onto his and blew into his mouth. She watched his chest to see if it rose. Nothing was happening so far.

Tunde held his breath; so did everyone else.

Simul8 tilted Tai-phoon's head back a little further and then blew into his mouth again.

Headspayce yelled, 'You gotta keep going!'

Simul8 yelled back, mid-breath, 'I'm the one who did the training course at school, dork brain.'

She breathed again into Tai-phoon's mouth, but there was no response.

Tunde intervened and he began pushing down on his chest to give CPR. There was a gurgling noise and then, suddenly, Tai-phoon was spouting water with his head to the side. Everyone cheered and chanted, 'Tunde! Simul8! Tunde! Simul8!'

Tai-phoon sat up and shrugged, 'Just swallowed some water, that's all. No biggie.'

But everyone was happy no matter what he said.

Simul8 was the happiest anyone had ever seen her.

Tunde knelt next to Tai-phoon, and said, 'You did it, Tai-phoon. You did it.'

Meanwhile, Yetie stared at the water-damaged door for several moments and then abruptly headbutted the water-logged computer screen in frustration. The glass exploded and a mini arc of electricity SPARKED and FIZZED and PHUTZED. The door slowly but surely slid open and then the sopping, drenched and exhausted cohort of kids filed out into yet another 'fun-filled' room designed to trap, damage or explode them.

Simul8 came up next to Tunde and said, softly, 'I'm sorry I panicked in there. Water makes me do that. I owe you.'

Tunde understood. 'Everybody's scared sometimes. And no one more than me – I was shaking like a jellyfish using a jackhammer.'

Simul8 laughed. It was a great sound.

J ust as Tunde and his new-found friends thought they might actually escape, Professor Shapiro appeared on a large screen with a familiar smirk on her lips. 'Poor you, all drenched and sodden. How cute that you'd think you could escape **The Complex.** Ha!'

No one responded.

Tunde looked around. This room didn't have any obvious escape routes. He whispered to Simul8 and Headspayce, 'Any ideas?'

Headspayce hissed in his ear, 'I've been in this room before. It's all about puzzles in here.'

And he was right. Professor Shapiro's superior

smirk disappeared and soon there was a picture of a cake filling the screen. Most of it had been eaten; there were only four pieces left.

Simul8 was breathing in for five and out for five. Her **Aargh!**-meter had strayed all the way back up to **Aaaaaaagh!** 'What is this supposed to mean? I don't understand. I preferred it in the other room. At least we knew it was going to end at some point.'

Tunde studied the picture intensely and then looked at Headspayce, who was slowly recovering from being dunked repeatedly like a digestive biscuit. They spoke simultaneously.

'This is . . . maths!'

But, before they could say anything else, the walls and ceiling began closing in. A wall panel slid open, revealing a numbered keyboard. Headspayce yelled at Tunde, 'I'm guessing we'll have to work out the answers and then type them in there before the room **crushes** us into a hamburger patty.'

And as he said that, the walls and floor and ceiling SCRUNCHED EVEN CLOSER TOGETHER. Yetie pushed hard against it, but the force and pressure was too much.

Tunde was drenched and overwhelmed. He moaned, 'I wish Jiah was here – she'd absolutely smash this!'

But it didn't matter, Headspayce had taken over: 'OK – there's a picture of four segments of cake. It's the last four bits of cake – last four bits of cake? What does that mean? Wait a minute – that's not a cake, that's a pie. The last four bits of pi . . . but pi is infinite. It's a trick question.'

Headspayce hit the keyboard and the symbol for infinity appeared. There was a flash, snap and crackle and a POP on the screen and then they were on to the next question!

It was the word INTEGER and there was a cymbal from a drum kit next to it.

Headspayce shouted at Tunde – 'It's the letter Z. They use Z as a *symbol* to represent integers. Don't ask me what it means, though.'

The walls and ceiling and floor scrunched in even further. Tai-phoon and Yetie were trying to push them apart. It was no use.

Simul8 piped up with, 'Numbers in German is "*Zahlen*".'

Headspayce typed the word Zahlen and the screen flashed green and a large tick appeared and Professor Shapiro's voice said, 'YOU'RRRREEEE RIGHT!'

However, the room was even smaller now, putting pressure on the larger members of the gang, particularly Yetie, who was once more trying to push the walls back with all her might. The room had stopped moving for a moment and (what Tunde hoped was) the final picture appeared on the screen. It was an octopus with the number eight over its head.

Tunde sat down. He had no idea what this question meant. Also, he was uncomfortable. His feet were soaking wet. He took off his shoes and revealed his socks. Which just so happened to be Jiah's gift from last Christmas.

Mathsox.

He looked at them and saw just by his big toe a similar equation to the one on the screen. He blurted

it out. 'The octo numbering system has a range of eight digits, type in zero to seven, so we can all get on with our lives.'

The walls, floor and ceiling began to close in even further and Backflash kept yelling, 'If only my powers were working, I could put us back by thirty seconds and we could survive this.'

The whole room of soon-to-be-squished kids

replied: 'BACKFLASH, SHUT UP!'

Headspayce was carefully typing in the numbers.
0 . . . **1** . . . **2** . . . **3** . . .

'Hurry up!' Simul8 bellowed at him. 'I can't bear it. This tree's branches are right in my face.'

Headspayce snapped back, 'Please be quiet, I'm trying to remember where I was and you're not helping.'

He continued the sequence and, finally, just as the walls, ceiling and floor of this horrible room were about to puree everyone within their grip **4** . . . **5** . . . **6** . . . **7** . . .

All movement stopped.

Everyone cheered.

A golden pass key rose from the floor. It was perched on a little podium. Tunde swiped it against the computer pad next to the closed doorway and it **SHIFFFFED** open and they all rushed through the door, determined to confront Professor Shapiro. Tunde led the way. He wanted his powers back and he wasn't going to take no for an answer.

14

While the superkids were busy fighting for their lives, Artie, who was usually a very patient android/robot/cyborg/artificial intelligence (take your pick) pretending to be a real boy, was becoming a trifle *im*patient. He had told Professor Krauss, after the earlier phone call with Professor Shapiro, that in his opinion something was terribly wrong. When Tunde had yelled at them on the phone, his levels – heart, blood, hydration, adrenaline – were **OFF THE CHARTS** and Artie had been very worried. If being chased by a rabid wolverine armed with swords, a bazooka and a hairdryer turned up to eleven made your heart beat at 200 beats per minute, then Tunde

must be in grave danger, because his was beating at 215 beats per minute.

Also, Professor Shapiro had sounded like she was being extra-persuasive with Professor Krauss, reassuring, calming – almost like a hypnotic snake with GOOGLY eyes. The way she spoke on the phone was mesmerizing, but as Artie was non-human, these techniques did not work on him. He sneakily typed what he knew about Professor Shapiro into S.H.I.P.P.E.'s (Sentient Hyper-Intelligent Pan-Planetary Entity) computer. This was a massive search engine that made Google look like a badly made abacus, designed by aliens determined to win any battle due to their superior smarty-pants knowledge.

Super quickly Artie read everything he could find about Professor Shapiro: gazillions of pages of information about her from around the world. He knew her parents worked for the government. She was a straight A+ student. Anything below an A+ meant an Everest of chores and all-night study sessions until she'd learnt her lessons. She left university with so many degrees and diplomas her parents had to hire a van and she had more letters after her name than there were in the alphabet. She was a valued advisor to the government because of her interest in global peace, which had led her to studying superpowered beings around the world. She had led a brigade of talented staff in observing and testing her young superpowered pupils and tried to isolate exactly what it was that made them *so* super.

The more Artie read, the more concerned he was that something fishy was going on. It was time for him to help Tunde. He hoped he'd be in time.

★

Professor Krauss sat at the head of a long table in a dark basement in Canary Wharf. He was talking to a very specialized group of scientists, all of whom were fascinated by his work at **The Facility,** his experiences with the two alien species, the Aviaans and the Furleenians, and also his prevention of World Wars Three, Four and Five within the last six months with the help of Tunde Wilkinson, the Boy with Wings. As he gave them the broad strokes of what he had experienced with Tunde (he didn't tell them everything, obviously; although they were trusted colleagues, he didn't trust anyone that much), his mind wandered a little.

He was mainly thinking about the phone call he had received from Tunde earlier, but every time he tried to think about it, Professor Shapiro's face would fill his head. Her eyes glowed, swirled and wobbled hypnotically, calming him down so that he felt more chilled than a polar bear sitting on the air-conditioning unit in an ice-cream van. He stopped thinking about how upset Tunde had sounded on the phone, and just concentrated on telling the scientists everything he could remember about the Boy with Wings. His colleagues nodded and took notes.

Ron and Ruth Wilkinson were watching *The Lion King* for the fifth time. They didn't know why they kept going, but they did. They really enjoyed it. They now knew the words so well, if one of the cast members had suddenly keeled over with bronchitis, either one of them could have stepped in and hollered out 'Hakuna Matata' big style to an adoring audience. They were surviving on popcorn and chewy sweets and fizzy pop.

Their phones were no longer working and they didn't question it at all, because when Professor Shapiro had waved them goodbye, she had also looked at them so deeply, her eyes growing huge and round, turning from red to yellow to blue to pink to orange and swirling, whirling and twirling round and round and round and in and out. She did say something about 'a season ticket to any musical for as long as

you wanted', 'sleep not being necessary' and also 'you won't even notice that Tunde has gone' and they were perfectly happy to sit there singing about life being a circle, about feeling the love tonight and also not being able to wait to be king. They sang along, ate ice cream, drank fizzy pop, passed out, woke up and did the whole thing **again** and **again** and **again.** And neither of them thought this was weird at all.

Back at **The Complex,** Tunde and his fellow students were swarming up a ladder to Professor Shapiro's observation room. Mid-swarm, Tunde turned to face his new friends, 'All the guards have gone. That means we've got a much better chance of getting hold of the zapper, regaining our powers and getting Shapiro and taking her to **The Facility** so that Professor Krauss can figure out what to do with her.'

Yetie argued, 'If I see this woman, I tweak off her nose!'

Backflash agreed. 'Aye. Good idea! Taking people's powers like that. She's a bully.'

Headspayce had been thinking long and hard. 'Maybe when *she* was a kid, she always wanted powers? Like somebody wanting to have the shiniest hair or perfect skin or the coolest bike in the school?'

Tunde added, 'Yeah, if you are at school and someone's got something you haven't, like perfect teeth or *friends*, you can drive yourself mad with jealousy.'

Simul8 yelled out, 'Just to remind you, we are all halfway up a ladder and Professor Shapiro is up there smirking at us right now.'

With that, they continued to climb, hopped in through an open window and soon found themselves facing Professor Shapiro, who was now wearing fancy flying goggles and a battle suit, complete with high-tech jetpack.

'I have to hand it to you, children, you're all much cleverer than I gave you credit for. But then that doesn't give you much credit. I'm so much cleverer than all of you put together. I am so much smarter than you, to even think **you** could defeat **me** would be like a teaspoon of frogspawn entering a pub quiz against Bill Gates, Einstein and a dolphin. You can never beat me. But thanks for trying, anyway.'

And now she held up the zapper triumphantly; this was the device that removed their powers and could reinstate them just as easily.

'In your short time here, you've given me all the information I need to give superpowers to myself and anyone else who'll pay the asking price. I'm going to be rich and, in a minute, you're going to be **gone.**'

She cackled like the green witch riding a broomstick in an old film about a girl in red shoes, a yappy puppy, a scaredy-cat, a rusty metal man and a raggedy, bendy bloke made of straw. They don't make them like that any more. She cackled again.

But Yetie had had enough. She crossed the room in three strides and slapped the zapper out of Professor Shapiro's hands. It spun in the air and Simul8 caught it safe and sound in her hands. She grinned.

Professor Shapiro bellowed, 'It doesn't matter whether you've got your powers or not, soon you'll be defunct, deleted and done! And good riddance, I don't need you any more.'

She pressed a button on her wrist unit (a large

bracelet with several buttons that glowed and pulsed mysteriously) and began hovering in mid-air. The ceiling opened above and Tunde saw blue sky for the first time in days. His heart leapt. But this was not the time for heart-leaping. Professor Shapiro was now moving upwards and upwards.

And they all watched helplessly, as she soared skyward, her jetpack propelling her to the roof, which had fully opened up like an enormous flower.

She shouted, 'So long, superkids. Enjoy being reduced to *ASHES*.' And she spoke into her face microphone – '**BEGIN COMPLEX SELF-DESTRUCT SEQUENCE NOW.**'

'**C**OMPLEX SELF-DESTRUCT SEQUENCE INITIATED: THE COMPLEX WILL SELF-DESTRUCT IN T-MINUS 60 SECONDS – 59, 58, 57 . . .'

The superkids were all completely shocked and had frozen in place as the remote robotic countdown continued noisily.

'38, 37, 36 . . .'

Tunde was **discombobulated**. Everyone huddled together. No one even tried to come up with a solution.

'32, 31, 30 . . .'

Tunde suddenly thought about his mum and dad and how gentle and kind they were. Yes, they were brilliant scientists. Yes, his dad told terrible jokes, but, most importantly, they had adopted him when he was an egg and they'd had no idea what would hatch from within. They were happy to wait and see and, since then, they'd looked after him, told him jokes, taught him right from wrong and how not to be a bully when he was easily the strongest and fastest kid in the whole school. Tunde loved his mum and dad for all those reasons.

He also loved his friends. Nev, because he was cool, but also kind and brilliant at scoring from the halfway line, in mid-air, and backwards. Dembe, because she was just like his sister. Also, she had his back at all times – usually because she'd just sellotaped a 'kick me' sign there. Kylie, because she said things like 'believe in yourself', 'do as you would be done by' and 'never fall asleep on a chocolate bar on a hot day'. And Jiah, his fellow nerd, who was as smart as a whip who had gone to Oxford, Cambridge **and** Harvard University. They were his best mates and he missed them.

'18, 17, 16 . . .'

Tunde looked at Headspayce who, right now, was shaking with fear. And then Tunde remembered that Simul8 had actually caught the remote control zapper thingy that would return everybody's powers, including his! He urgently asked her to pass it over, and then pressed the big metallic button and, with a

WHOOSH!

Multiple **BCREAKS!**

Several **BADOOFS!**

Everyone's powers were restored!

It was a great moment, right up there with landing on the moon, winning the gold medal for the 100 metres at the Olympics, and finding a fifty pound note on your way home from school. Everyone was cheering, thrilled to be feeling their powers again.

Simul8 had taken the form of an oak tree and was hugging Klara-Phill. Yetie was so excited, she shot thirty metres in the air and stayed there. Tunde released his wings and soared, swooped and slalomed around everyone else. He was beaming like a giant laser on its birthday, but it became very clear that time was running out.

'7, 6, 5 . . .'

And then Backflash leapt to his feet and shouted with triumph, **'FINALLY!'**

And he twirled his hands and did a little dance and, suddenly, the robotic voice rang out,

'34, 33, 32 . . .'

Backflash had done it! Tunde thanked him and then quickly grabbed a phone from Professor Shapiro's

desk. 'Now let's get out of here!' He punched some buttons and immediately began talking, 'Artie, listen—'

But then he was interrupted by a familiar voice:

'Stop talking and stay where you are!'

The countdown continued – **'7, 6, 5, 4 . . .'**

Backflash did his little jig once more and waved his hands once more and the countdown changed once more—

'34, 33, 32 . . .'

A beam of light shot down and every single superpowered kid was teleported into the body of S.H.I.P.P.E.!

'7, 6, 5, 4, 3, 2, 1 . . .'

There was a loud crumping noise as the underground **Complex** imploded. All those high-tech laboratories and super-complicated computers: all that hard work ***KER-CRUMPED, KABLOOYEED*** and ***KA-BLAOWED!***

With so many on board S.H.I.P.P.E., Tunde had to make a vital decision. As everyone else was being transported upwards and into the ship, Tunde flew towards the access window in the ceiling as fast as he possibly could.

Artie spoke to him through S.H.I.P.P.E.'s loudspeaker. 'Tunde, what are you doing?'

'You took your time. I'm gonna fly behind you. You've got too many guests on board.'

'But you need to be in *here*. We're flying above London in an alien spacecraft, chasing a crazy woman in a jetpack! You've got to be sensible.'

Tunde replied, 'That's the last thing I want to be. Being sensible is what got me here in the first place. Professor Shapiro needs to be stopped.'

And then, a familiar voice beamed from the speakers as Tunde flew alongside S.H.I.P.P.E. It was Nev.

'Bruv, you all right? Soon as Artie told us what was going down, we all said, "D'you know what? Rock climbing, banging tunes and the best virtual reality games we've ever played in our lives just can't compete with helping Tunde!" We're like family, innit?'

And then Dembe chimed in, 'Yeah, but you lot don't live with him. Me, Tunde and Artie have to laugh at Mr Wilkinson's *terrible* jokes whether we like it or not.'

Tunde laughed, but then looked down. They were flying low and at speed and Tunde spotted the British Library, the British Museum and Trafalgar Square.

Tourists looked up into the sky and pointed at this extraordinary sight. Tunde couldn't imagine what they thought they were seeing – but a large alien spacecraft, chockfull of superpowered kids, flown by an android led by a boy with wings, hell-bent on battling a mad professor who just wants to leap a tall building with a single bound, run faster than a speeding bullet and fly like an angel probably *wasn't* it. It wasn't just extraordinary, it was super-ultra-hyper-mega-straordinary!

Thanks to the earpod system of S.H.I.P.P.E., Tunde could hear what was going on inside as he zipped along.

'Oh, I see,' Headspayce said. 'This is a kind of anti-grav teleporter module. Or it could be a superstring kaleidoscopic warp-winder. I would assume all these lights and blobs and bleeps are a kind of system monitor facility.'

Kylie wheeled up and pointed to everything: 'You're wrong. That's a microwave oven, that's a washing machine and the lights are just for when people want to go to the toilet. Nice try, though.'

Yetie laughed her head off at this and gave Klara-Phill a loud high five, so thunderous it almost snapped off one of her branch-like arms. But, miraculously, in the bubbling mass of green goo, the limb grew back instantly and as good as new.

Jiah shook her head. 'Nature is one thing, but supernature is **ultra-megatastic!**'

Tunde couldn't help smile at this. But that vanished when Professor Shapiro swivelled around and saw S.H.I.P.P.E. and Tunde steadily gaining . . .

She yelled back at him, 'Oh no. Oh no, no, no, no, no. This is *not* how this ends. Don't you kids understand? *Whatever* this space blob is and whoever's inside, whether you've got powers or not, you can't stop me. We're nearly there now. And no one's going to forget this, whoever they are, wherever they live in the world.'

Tunde soared across to her. 'We **can** stop you. All my friends are here now, and we'll do it together. But you know who else can stop you? You! You must realize, you can't just keep doing mean things because you're stronger or smarter or have powers. If you're lucky enough to have those things, you should use them to help others.'

Professor Shapiro laughed. 'Help others? **What others?** You mean those little guys down there? This will all be over so quickly, they won't even know what hit them. I've got the powers, Tunde; the ones that count anyway. Simul8's and yours. It's delightful that you followed me and put all your new friends in one place.'

And she took off her jetpack and let it fall hundreds of metres to the ground. Then she began to fall. It was all quite sudden.

Tunde yelled, 'I'll catch you, don't worry.'

But Professor Shapiro laughed and pressed the device on her wrist. She sprouted wings, huge golden beautiful wings, like an eagle's, but supersized. She was cloning Tunde.

'You see, with Simul8's cloning power and the added attraction of your wings and the **spooky-ooky**

Blackfire, I don't *need* anyone to catch me. In fact, if you can catch me, good luck. I'm going to blast the House of Commons to $SMITHEREENS$ and someone very important on the other side of the world is going to pay a gazillion dollars into my bank account. Ain't life grand? Bye.'

And she soared towards the House of Commons and Big Ben.

16

Tunde had FROZEN in mid-air.

Headspayce was suddenly in his mind, panicking. 'She's got Simul8's powers, which means she can copy anything anybody can throw at her. She's got your wings and your Blackfire powers. From what you've told me, that makes her pretty undefeatable. What are we going to do?'

Jiah piped up, 'There has to be a solution to this. Without the jetpack, she's slowed down a little as she learns to use her – I mean, Tunde's – wings. That gives us time.'

'And when we get to her, I can reset time to thirty seconds ago!' Backflash chimed in. 'If that's any help.'

Tunde yelled, 'Everybody has to follow me. Headspayce, you've given me an idea. Simul8, are you there?'

There was a kerfuffle in the ship and then, suddenly, the super-mimic was on loudspeaker.

'Tunde, I'm here and present and correct. What do you need?'

And then he told her.

And she laughed, like a particularly noisy drain. 'I'm loving your work, Mr Wilkinson. Let us go and get that nutty professor and give her a taste of her own medicine.'

Tunde soared ahead as fast as he could and S.H.I.P.P.E. followed.

Simul8 had quickly joined Tunde flying ahead of S.H.I.P.P.E. – they were making short work of the distance between them and Professor Shapiro. Simul8 enjoyed the whole flying process so much, she couldn't keep a big silly grin off her face.

'This is the best thing ever. I should just copy birds all day. Imagine: you're miles in the air; you get a bird's-eye view of everything. Anyone down there gets on your nerves, you just poop on their head! Genius!' She flew through a cohort of pigeons and laughed as they scattered to and fro.

Tunde put on a stern face. 'Simul8, this is serious! Shapiro wants to blow up the House of Commons and Big Ben. She says she has my powers and yours. We've got to stop her. Did you do exactly as I said?'

Simul8 nodded, banked to the right majestically, then CORKSCREWED and, at the last minute, overtook Tunde, who laughed out loud at her cheek.

'But if it's a race you want, let's do this. The first one to Shapiro gets to save the world.'

And it wasn't just them now. Soon, there were film camera crews from all over the world jostling for a view, and camera drones rising up from the crowds. The words on everybody's lips were 'Are they going to hurt us?', 'Do they want to take us captive?' and 'Dem wings are sick, I wonder how much they cost?'

★

181

Beneath the House of Commons in the high-powered meeting rooms situated several floors below ground level, the Prime Minister and his advisors discussed who should be given the job of vanquishing this superhuman threat.

Luckily for Tunde and everyone else, the first person the Prime Minister called was Professor Krauss, who had now recovered, thankfully, from being hypnotized by Professor Shapiro and was no longer behaving like a soppy lovesick empty-headed booby. He was absolutely PIN-SHARP now and ready to give Shapiro a taste of her own medicine using a high-tech Facility communication device (the Fac-One mobile phone).

'Artie, um, perhaps we should put S.H.I.P.P.E. into cloak-mode? You're getting rather a lot of attention, flying an alien spaceship across London. What do you think?' Professor Krauss said.

'Oops.'

Suddenly, the ship disappeared from view, confusing an entire legion of news, government and

RAF spectators, all of whom were now questioning their sanity.

Professor Krauss continued, 'Excellent, m'boy. Now, does Tunde have a plan?'

Jiah answered on Artie's behalf, 'According to myself, Artie and a rather charming person called Headspayce – not the spelling you're used to – yes, there is a plan. Tunde told Nev to, and I quote, "Leave it with me and Sim, bruv, we've got this" and signed off. Apparently . . . it's going to be a "doozy".'

Professor Krauss thanked her and hung up. He then turned to the Prime Minister. 'Everything's under control, Prime Minister. They say it's going to be a "doozy".'

A general rushed in, wearing more medals than Krauss had ever seen in his entire life. 'Sorry to interrupt, Prime Minister, sah! There's a woman with wings hovering near Big Ben, sah! She is being pursued by a boy *and* a girl, *both* of whom also appear to possess wings, sah! There have been sightings of some kind of alien spaceship, but that seems to have

disappeared, sah! Permission to blast all of them away from sovereign territory and then have a nice lie-down, sah! My nerves are in tatters, sah!'

Professor Krauss interrupted him before he could say anything else, 'Prime Minister, may I suggest you give the boy and his friend a chance, so that we can all see what he's made of. He's only thirteen, but he's been training for this his whole life. I don't think you'll be disappointed.'

The Prime Minister looked at Krauss's face carefully: there was kindness there. Also, a youthfulness, which was odd, because Krauss had been advising successive governments since just after World War Two, yet his skin was mostly unlined and his back was straight and he appeared to have all his marbles.

The Prime Minister pulled himself together. 'Of course. Let's see what the lad can do.'

And so they held their breath and watched, waited and prayed that the boy with wings would come up trumps.

While they did, one hundred metres above Big Ben, Professor Shapiro, Simul8 and Tunde faced each other.

'I'm actually glad you kids are here, because now you'll see what you should actually do with your powers – instead of running away to London and playing at being your favourite hero, you should be setting yourself up for life. Once I'm done blowing Big Ben and the House of Commons to S𝑀ITHEREENS, I'll be able to do anything and go anywhere I want. This is going to be so much fun.'

And Professor Shapiro began to **power up.** Tunde could see the energy crackling round and through her entire system. She was building up to using the Blackfire. He was more than a little terrified. But he also trusted the plan.

'Shapiro, you said you want our powers and that's all you want? Isn't that kinda stupid?'

Simul8 started taunting. 'Yeah, why just take **our** powers? Only two skill sets instead of all of them. If it was me—'

Professor Shapiro bristled.

'But, thankfully, I'm not you. Unlike you, I don't just have half a brain. We ran comprehensive tests on all of you. Some of you are still an unknown quantity. I made a judgement call as to which power set suited me best. It would have been careless to take everybody's powers. The outcome would be unpredictable, to say the least.'

Simul8 looked at Tunde and yawned. 'Now?'

Tunde nodded.

And then, suddenly, Simul8 soared across the airspace **WOOOOOOOOOOOOOOOOOOSHHHH!** And then pressed the big metal button of the Power Leech device. What Shapiro didn't know was that Professor Krauss, Jiah and Headspayce had worked together and had managed to alter the mechanics of this ingenious power stealing doo-hickey to completely REVERSE its effects. Rather than *taking* powers now, it *transferred* them. So, when Simul8 **ZAPPED** Shapiro, she pushed ALL the rest of the kids' powers directly into Professor Shapiro in one long **SZHOINNNNNNNNNNNNNNNNNNNNNN-NNNNNNNNNNNNNNNNNNNNNNK!**

This was the moment when it all got ugly.

Professor Shapiro abruptly exploded with branch-like limbs, green goo shot from her eyes, she kept changing size, suddenly it rained, snowed, she shot hailstones from her nostrils, she was furious! Every so often, there'd be a noise, **BOOMF!** And all her transformations from the last thirty seconds would reverse and then start again.

'**WHAT IS HAPPENING TO MEEEEEEE?**' she screamed and added for good measure, 'The human system can't bear this amount of mutation!'

Tunde replied, 'You said you wanted all the power. This is everything you wished for!'

Professor Shapiro shrank to a quarter of an inch tall, then grew super quickly to a height of forty metres and a width of thirty metres. She then grew roots from her feet, and mammoth branches from her shoulders. And finally, the Blackfire expanded and grew and shone like an eclipse gone mad and completely consumed her in a ball of black flame.

She was GONE.

There was a long government broadcast that night. It beamed from every radio station across the British Isles and the rest of the world. The Prime Minister was talking about a closely averted terrorist attack on the people of Great Britain and kept repeating certain phrases about 'allies', 'friends' and 'rescue'. There was also some strange but beautiful music playing the entire time he spoke.

What no one in the world knew or understood was that the entire broadcast was designed by Professor Krauss and his colleagues at **The Facility**. The combination of musical passages and key words and certain mix of visual imagery had been created as a

mass-hypnotic tool to wipe everyone's memory. Anyone who had seen a spaceship or two flying kids or a woman with wings change size repeatedly, become a tree for five seconds and then do it all again, every single person who had seen or heard about these things, would no longer remember them.

Tunde's mum and dad immediately came out of their trance-like stupor. They couldn't wait to hug Tunde – and they didn't want to see another musical for a long, long time.

Almost immediately, Tunde and all his friends were swept to Buckingham Palace to receive medals from the King. Everyone was very proud of themselves. Even Klara-Phill, who didn't really understand the concept of medals and kept getting annoyed when palace staff kept sweeping up her leaves and branches as she had taken root whilst waiting for her medal.

Tunde, Simul8, Artie and Professor Krauss were all given the George Medal for Bravery. Ron and Ruth almost passed out with joy. Tunde was a true hero. The King shook everyone's hand and talked privately with Tunde and Professor Krauss about how important it was that someone like Tunde would take on all-comers like that and protect the country. Tunde blushed. He'd never been complimented by royalty before.

Simul8 was also congratulated, but was very nervous and, as the King approached, she became an exact copy of him, then the Queen Consort, then a Beefeater, *then* a corgi and, finally, herself again. The

entire room clapped. Simul8 looked embarrassed, but the King thanked her for the entertainment.

Afterwards, they were given a tour of London they would never forget. Everyone was allowed a starter, main meal and dessert in three different restaurants. They all wanted burgers, fish and chips, hot dogs, Chinese and Indian. The Prime Minister had laid down the law and insisted that one of his Special Assistants make sure that these brave kids got whatever they requested. They went around on electric scooters, visiting the different London sights. Packing in as many experiences as they could until it was time to eat again!

Tunde, Artie, Nev, Jiah, Dembe and Kylie sat at the top table surrounded by all their new friends in the basement at Downing Street. Krauss was on the other end, busy talking to government officials. There were lots of good things to eat.

Nev spoke for everybody. 'We shouldn't have let you go to London to **The Complex.**'

Tunde shook his head. 'It wasn't your fault. I thought I was doing the right thing. And I was; but it turned out I wasn't. Professor Shapiro wasn't who she said she was.'

Professor Krauss jumped in here and added, 'It turns out Professor Shapiro had been a master spy on the global troublemaking circuit. She'd been using our resources to investigate how to transfer superpowers for the evil purpose of enhancing specially chosen soldiers and releasing them onto the world's battlefields. Worst thing about it all was that she was only in it for the money!'

Tunde sighed, 'You know, when I first arrived I was feeling sorry for myself. I thought I was on my own. And it's so weird because, that just wasn't true. Wherever I was and whatever I was doing, you guys were with me all the time in my head!

'Nev, you helped me cope in the first test. Kylie, your wisdom helped me to make friends.

'Dembe, I even tried to do your natural swagger and made a fool of myself.'

Dembe shrugged and gave a sly grin. 'This kinda swag don't come easy, bruv. You get me?'

'And, Jiah,' Tunde continued, 'we would have been squished to bits if I hadn't been wearing the Mathsox.'

Headspayce practically leapt across the table to speak to her. 'Jiah, we would have been smooshed to pizza without the Mathsox. Any time you want to buy me a gift like that for any reason – I'm happy. I salute you. You should be a professor in your own right.'

Jiah blushed, muttered something like, 'I will be,

don't worry,' under her breath and everybody in the room laughed and clapped.

It was a very happy time. And Tunde looked around – at his old friends, his new superfriends, his parents and Professor Krauss – and thought if only it could just stay like this forever, it would be the best. And for a little while at least, it was.

The end.

Acknowledgements

A big thank you to everyone creatively involved in the book, including Keenon Ferrell, who is a legend, my editorial team, Sam, Gurnaik, Louisa, Amy, Rachel, and the whole team at Macmillan Children's Books.

Also to my family, The Henrys and The Parkers, to lovely Lisa, Billie and, of course, Esme.

About the Author

Sir Lenny Henry has risen from being a star on children's television to becoming one of Britain's best-known comedians, as well as a writer, philanthropist and award-winning actor. He is also co-founder of the charity Comic Relief. Lenny is a strong advocate for diversity and has recently co-written the book *Access All Areas: The Diversity Manifesto for TV and Beyond.*

About the Illustrator

Keenon Ferrell is an illustrator and animator based in New York. He makes artwork inspired by music, fashion and sports. He also has a love for storytelling, fantasy and history which can be seen throughout his work. Keenon's clients include: Netflix, Capital One, StoryCorps and Sony Music Entertainment, to name a few.

Also available by Lenny Henry:

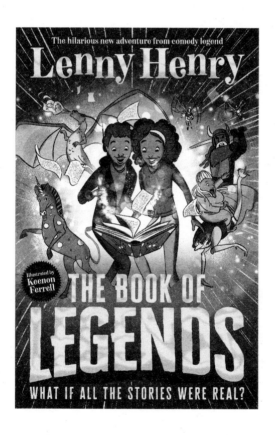

Missed Tunde's first Extraordinary Adventure? Turn the page for a chapter of *The Boy With Wings*

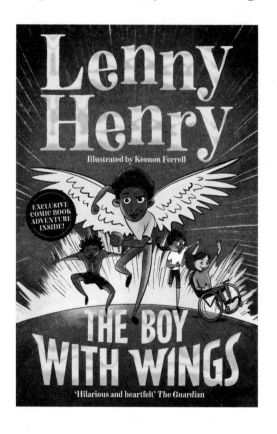

Prologue

The magpie perched on the window ledge and peered through the glass, as if binge-watching its favourite television programme. The bird had abandoned its constant search for beetles, flies, caterpillars, spiders and worms (imagine that lot in a pie . . .). Right now, it just wanted to observe the boy.

The magpie had no idea why it wanted to watch the boy; it only knew that it was very, very important that it did. And so the busy-body bird stayed there on the sill, all the while keeping its shining dark eyes on him.

1
TUNDE IS TWELVE!

It was Tunde's twelfth birthday. He was having a party – a modest celebration with a few friends. He was looking forward to it and had no idea, not the slightest clue or faintest inkling, that it would end with a massive, knock-'em-down, fingers-up-the-nostrils, hair-pulling, nose-squishing BRAWL.

A few things to know about Tunde before we get going: Tunde was adopted.

He had no idea who his birth parents were or why they'd given him up. And he didn't much care either.

Well . . . that's what Tunde told his friends anyway. The truth about how he really felt about being adopted was BENDIER and TWISTIER than a rubber band in a microwave.

Tunde's adopted mum and dad were called Ron and Ruth Wilkinson, and Tunde was very happy with them.

They were cool.

For a start – they looked like him. They were dark skinned, Caribbean, but British born. They were hard-working, intelligent and loved him through and through. Tunde's mum, Ruth, was tall, had an epic Afro hairdo that she pulled back into a humongous bun (so big it could be seen from the moon, his dad would say) and gorgeous dark skin. She worked at a laboratory called **The Facility**, where she spent days staring at multiple screens, trying to get her computers to talk to each other. That was how she explained her job to Tunde, at least.

Ron Wilkinson was shorter than his wife. He had black curly hair, most of it on his head, but some SPROUTED from his ears and the neck of his shirt. He often joked about being part sheepdog. Ron also worked at **The Facility**, which is where he and Ruth had met. Ron's job involved taking fruit and veg and nuts and berries and seeds and, through scientific means, trying to make them bigger, stronger, more nutritious and tastier.

He enjoyed his work and often brought super-sized samples home with him. A marrow he'd winched through the window, the enormous blueberry that had to stay in the garden, the talking Atlantic salmon that lived in the bath for a while.

Tunde had never been inside **The Facility** but he had walked past it loads. It was famous in the neighbourhood. All the laboratories and testing grounds were surrounded by walls, fences and barbed wire, just like Scrooge McDuck's wallet.

Tunde got picked on a lot – at school, on the bus, even playing in the park – mostly because of the colour of his skin, so his mum and dad made sure to teach him about some of the great and successful people – inventors, explorers, athletes, doctors, nurses, scientists, and musicians – who looked exactly like him.

If anyone called him a horrible name at school, they told Tunde to think of:

- Benjamin Banneker, an inventor who'd made a clock that kept perfect time for forty years.
- Muhammad Ali, who'd won the boxing heavyweight world championship three times in a row.

- Dr Martin Luther King, Jr., who'd marched and braved high-powered water hoses and vicious dogs in order to gain freedom for people who looked like Tunde.
- And . . . Garrett Morgan, the bloke who invented the traffic light.

Tunde remembered them all, but he still found it difficult not to cry when he was picked on by name-calling hooligans with fewer brain cells than a potato.

Knowing the name and achievements of a boxer doesn't mean you can beat the biggest bully in your year in a fight (at Tunde's school this was Quinn Patterson). It just means you've got a good memory.

Whenever Tunde tried to explain this to his dad, Ron would say, 'Son, there's a time when you have to stand up for what's right. Sometimes the only way to deal with a bully is to bonk 'em once, hard on the beezer. That'll teach 'em a lesson.'

Then he'd cackle like a mad wizard, point to his nose, **squidge** it and go, 'HONK HONK!'

Tunde didn't want to bonk anybody on the beezer,

partly because he wasn't that keen on violence and partly because he didn't want to get into trouble. Still, he appreciated the advice.

Sometimes his dad would try and cheer him up with a terrible joke. For instance, if Tunde felt sad, Ron would scratch his head, hitch up his pants and say:

Knock, knock.

Who's there?

Candice.

Candice who?

Candice door open soon, I'm dyin' for a wee!

There were more where that came from; some of Ron's other favourite jokes included:

Why did the apple turnover?

Because he couldn't get to sleep.

Or:

What did the mummy tomato say to the baby tomato that was

lagging behind?

Ketchup!

Tunde never found them quite as funny as his dad did, but seeing him roar with laughter at his own jokes made Tunde happy.

The truth was, Tunde got on well with his mum and dad. His life, aside from Quinn Patterson and his gang of smelly yobboes, was good.

Even so, sometimes those **TWISTY**, *MELTY*, rubber-band-in-a-microwave feelings about being adopted would niggle away at him and he'd have to push them down inside. Anyway, back to Tunde's twelfth birthday, and the party that would end in a massive brawl that would make even Muhammad Ali proud.

Party day began bright and sunny. Tunde's mum had gone to **LOADS** of effort – frying, baking, steaming, slicing, dicing. As usual, there was **WAY TOO MUCH** food and, knowing Tunde's mum's cooking, quite a bit of it would be inedible.

Tunde had invited his best friends from school: Kylie

Collins, Jiah Patel and Nev Carter. Just three guests. They could all fit into a shoebox if pushed.

Kylie Collins rocked a wheelchair, had perfect aim with a bow and arrow, and her mum was a relationship counsellor. Kylie often repeated things she'd heard her mum say at work, such as: 'Don't just say how you feel: show it!'

And:

'The height of madness is doing the same thing over and over and expecting a different result.'

And, best of all:

'If you're going to fight, fight productively!'

Jiah Patel, who was very practical, thought this last one was particularly high-larious. 'Brilliant, so if I'm being pummelled by maniac zombies, I should build a Lego model of Disney World? Productivity in action!'

Jiah was a mathlete. She didn't care what anyone thought about her . . . apart from her parents, that is. As far as they were concerned, school was one big, bloodthirsty, no-holds-barred competition and if you weren't in it, no way could you win it.

Jiah wore glasses, had read every comic book ever, sometimes went on a bit, and was the kindest person they knew. Even so, Kylie and Tunde were no longer shy about telling her to put a sock in it.

Then, there was the GUEST OF HONOUR, the Coolest Guy in the School (perhaps the entire universe!) in Tunde's eyes: Nev Carter!

Nev was fit as a flea; the kind of flea that works out three times a day and does yoga at the weekend. They hadn't been friends that long, but they'd hit it off big-time. Tunde had been praying feverishly that Nev would attend the party. He didn't want to be the only boy there. That would be major league awkward. Tunde would then be crowned the King of Awk-land. He shuddered at the thought.

Tunde helped his parents set out the various party foods on a trestle table by the kitchen door, then excitedly waited for the guests to arrive.

Kylie got there first. Her taxi screeched to a halt by the front gate and, once she'd told the driver off for speeding, she zipped into the garden.

'Whoa! Tunde, your garden's **GINORMOUS!** You could land two 747s sideways in that allotment, I'm not even jokin'!' She wasn't wrong. The Wilkinsons had a vast lawn, an orchard of fruit trees, and a picture-perfect allotment. The garden, with its clever and precise landscaping, was entirely down to Tunde's dad's new-found obsession with gardening.

It had all started when he'd been passed over for promotion *yet again*. The powers that be just didn't think super-sized, super-tasty fruit and veg were that important.

Ron told everyone that he didn't mind being overlooked yet again, even though his face told a different story – but shortly afterwards, he started doing a lot of gardening.

In the last year, Ron had spent nearly all his spare time mowing, trimming, cutting and strimming, clipping, pruning, planting, fine-tuning, raking, hoeing, composting and sowing.

The garden used to be completely wild, so bad Amazon explorers would have given up at the front gate. Tunde had overheard his mum a gazillion times saying things like:

'Well, I'd like to go out and hang the washing, but I'd

need a map and a massive machete to get there.' Or she might say:

'Ron, I'm heading to bed – and, just for a change, I won't use the stairs. I'll use the fifty foot of ivy that's growing through the cracks in our walls . . .'

So, when Ron started organizing the garden in an obsessive way, Ruth was thrilled. At first. However, after a while, this mania had become . . . a bit much. Both Tunde and his mum hoped Dad would finally get a promotion at **The Facility.** Then maybe he would stop trimming the hedge with nail scissors.

Now, as Kylie whizzed up and down the garden's various, neatly mapped pathways exclaiming, 'Dude, did your dad do all this with a big ruler?' Nev and Jiah arrived, bearing gifts.

Although this was his twelfth birthday, an age when a lot of kids turn their backs on childish things like Father Christmas, the Easter Bunny and things like that, Tunde loved getting presents! He tore the Sellotape off with his teeth, just to get a look at his swag.

. . . to be continued . . .